What the critics are saying

"Treat yourself to this delicious concoction...if you are fond of reading erotica, and want a good story with lots of twists and turns, then, by all means, grab a copy of SEIZED, a great futuristic novel." - *Robin Taylor, In The Library*

"SEIZED definitely lives up to expectations. Well- written and full of spicy hot sex, the book easily returns to the cultures and events that captured our attention in the first book, while expanding on Dak and Geris' romance enough to make the story both new and intriguing." - *Ann Leveille, Sensual Romance Reviews*

Ellora's Cave Publishing, Inc.

Discover for yourself why readers can't get enough of the multiple award-winning publisher Ellora's Cave. Whether you prefer e-books or paperbacks, be sure to visit EC on the web at www.ellorascave.com for an erotic reading experience that will leave you breathless.

www.ellorascave.com

Trek Mi Q'an Series

- The Empress' New Clothes
- Seized
- No Mercy
- Enslaved
- No Escape
- Naughty Nancy (in anthology *Things That Go Bump In The Night*)
- No Fear
- Dementia (in anthology *Taken*)
- Lost in Trek I
- Devilish Dot (in anthology *Venus Is Burning*)
- Armageddon

Ellora's Cave Publishing, Inc.
PO Box 787
Hudson, OH 44236-0787

ISBN # 0-9724377-3-8

Edited by Martha Punches.
Cover art by Darrell King.

Warning: The following material contains strong sexual content meant for mature readers. *Seized* has been rated NC17, erotic, by three independent reviewers. We strongly suggest storing this book in a place where young readers not meant to view it are unlikely to happen upon it. That said, enjoy…

SEIZED

A Trek Mi Q'an Tale

Written by

Jaid Black

WARNING:

Seized cannot be read without first reading its predecessor,
The Empress' New Clothes.

To Sherri L. King for demanding Geris have her own story.

"What is a friend? A single soul dwelling in two bodies."
                                    - *Aristotle*

Prologue
The Catskill Mountains

"Sweet Jesus in heaven, I'm losing my damn mind."

Her eyes unblinking, Geris Jackson mumbled her thoughts in a monotone voice as she plunked into the black leather driver's seat of her BMW. Freshly recovered from a fainting spell, she decided that she had hallucinated the events leading up to it. She had to have.

Because no way had *that* happened, she thought, her jaw gone slack. No way had two gigantic men with glowing blue eyes kidnapped her best friend from the parking lot of *The Smiling Faces and Peaceful Hearts Meditation Retreat*. That was simply too ludicrous to believe. It sounded like a scenario straight from a sitcom—and a really cheesy one at that.

But if that was true and she had been dreaming or hallucinating, then where the hell was Kyra?

Geris nibbled on her lower lip, her almond-shaped eyes wide. "She must have gone to get me help," she murmured, her gaze slowly lifting to stare at herself in the rearview mirror. "You know, when you fainted, girl." She forced a nervous smile to her full African-inherited lips, as if that small gesture somehow made her barely audible words more credible to her ears.

Closing her eyes tightly, she took a deep, calming breath and slowly blew it out. *You were hallucinating,* she told herself over and over again. *You were hallucinating. And when you open your eyes everything will be back to normal.*

Drawing in another deep tug of air, Geris's light brown eyes flicked back open, her breath expelling in a rush. She stared at herself in the rearview mirror while she absently tucked a stray micro-braid behind an ear. "Get out of the car," she muttered to her image. "Get out of the car and go find Kyra."

Her hand trembling, she lifted it to the handle and slowly opened the driver's side door. Her heart beating wildly, her body feeling as heavy as lead, she lifted herself up on unsteady feet, terrified beyond reason that the hallucination hadn't been a hallucination and that her best friend was...

No.

She shook her head. No, the good lord above wouldn't do that to her, she told herself firmly. Because Kyra was all Geris had in this world and the ministers in church had always said God would never give a person more burden in life than they could bear.

Geris's mother was dead. Her father was dead. Kyra's younger sister Kara had disappeared a year ago without a trace, a young woman she had loved like her own sister. Geris had no siblings, no husband, no children, and no friends she felt connected to in the way she felt connected to Kyra.

Kyra was *not* dead, she resolutely decided, her hands clenching so tightly her fingernails dug into her palms to the point of pain. Nor was Kyra gone. She was here. She had to be here. Because if she wasn't here Geris would be all alone, separated from the woman she hadn't been separated from since kindergarten. And then what would she have?

Nothing.

For twenty-seven years Geris and Kyra had been all but joined at the hip, completely inseparable since the age of five. They had met in Miss Rocco's kindergarten class after Geris and her mother had moved from a trendy part of Harlem into a trendier part of Manhattan Island when her father died. Geris's mother, an actress, couldn't stand to be reminded of her dead husband and Geris, although only five years old, understood enough about what was going on around her to realize that her beloved mama was slowly fading away from her.

So she hadn't complained when the woman she loved more than life itself took her from all that she knew and moved away from the old neighborhood. All she cared about was pleasing her mama. And making her eyes light up again.

Only the move didn't help. And every day Hera Danelle Jackson faded away more and more until she was nothing but a ghost of her former self.

Five-year-old Geris had been lonely. She missed her daddy, wanted her mama back, and had no friends to play with at school. She felt different from the other kids, and was shy to boot, so finding playmates had been difficult.

But then a couple of months later something happened, something completely unexpected...

A chubby little redheaded girl from the Irish Bronx moved to Manhattan and into Miss Rocco's class. The girl was awkward and overweight, shoddily dressed (at least for Manhattan) and wore the ugliest coke-bottle glasses Geris Jackson had ever seen.

At first Geris hadn't paid the chubby little redhead much attention, for she didn't pay any of the kids much attention. But then one day on the playground when Geris was swinging as high as her swing would go, flying away from her life like a bird in the sky, she heard the Irish girl softly crying as some older kids shoved her into the dirt and called her mean names.

"Look at the fat kid cry!" a third-grade boy named Jimmy Paluchi taunted as he kicked the redheaded girl in the knee, breaking the skin. "Maybe if you weren't so fat and ugly you could fight back!"

The other boys laughed while Jimmy continued to mock her. The Irish girl didn't fight back, just sat there in the dirt and softly cried, looking as broken as Geris had felt ever since her daddy'd gone and died.

For as long as she lived Geris would never forget that moment. Like a freeze-frame, like a still portrait in time, she would always be able to recall Kyra's tear-stained cheeks, the terrified expression in the silver eyes that had been magnified through thick glasses, the way that her bottom lip quivered as the boys taunted her with cruel names...

Her nostrils flaring, a warbled sound of anger erupting from her throat, five-year-old Geris jumped off of the swing, landed on her feet, and flew as fast as her nimble legs would carry her toward Jimmy Paluchi. She jumped onto his back and began beating him with her tiny fists, feeling as out of control as a wild animal.

She continued to lash out at him, angrier than she could ever remember being, all of the emotions she hadn't known how to express since her daddy'd died erupting in one fierce burst of strength. She hit Jimmy Paluchi for her dead daddy, for her ghost of a mama, for herself—

And for the chubby little redheaded Irish girl with the ugly-as-sin glasses and banged up knee.

"Geris!" she heard Miss Rocco screech as she came running toward her. "Geris Jackson, stop this fighting at once!"

But try as she might, she couldn't stop. She hit Jimmy Paluchi with her tiny fists until they were numb, until two teachers pulled her off of the sobbing bully's back and forcibly carried her into the principal's office.

"You wait until your mother hears about this, young lady!"

Her mama had heard about it, she recalled. And sad though it was, even that incident hadn't been enough to snap her mother back to reality. The renowned Broadway actress Hera Jackson continued to die a bit more every day, and Geris reacted accordingly, withdrawing more and more into her five-year-old shell.

The memories were a bit fuzzy at the age of thirty-two, but the impressions of how alone she had felt were still poignant.

After the playground incident, Geris had seen Kyra in class, but never spoke to her. Later she would find out that Kyra's father had just died too and that her mother was as broken in spirit as Geris's was—a common bond that would forever unite the two women. But at five years of age, Geris couldn't see that. All she could see was that this girl she had defended, this girl she had gotten in trouble for, treated her as though she didn't exist. Just like her mama.

Roughly two weeks later, she was eating her lunch outside, sitting away from the others as she always did, when she heard footsteps coming up from behind her.

Geris frowned at the chubby redhead. "Whadda you want?" she asked gruffly, her almond-shaped eyes narrowed.

The Irish girl stopped dead in her tracks, her silver eyes wide. The girl hesitated for a moment as if deciding what to do, unknowingly giving Geris time to realize that she didn't want her to leave. Something inside told Geris she had done the wrong thing and her five-year-old heart knew she'd made the chubby girl feel as badly as her mama always made her feel.

Like nobody wanted her.

Geris frowned severely. She had a chip on her shoulder a mile wide by now and wasn't nobody gonna knock it off. "Well since y'here you might as well sit down." The girl plopped down on the ground beside her. Geris scowled. *"What's your name, anyway?"*

The chubby redhead pushed her coke-bottle glasses up the bridge of her nose. *"Kyra,"* she whispered, her childhood accent a mix of lilt and the Bronx. She cleared her throat. *"You're Geris. I heard Miss Rocco say that."*

Geris nodded.

"You wanna be best friends?"

And that quickly the chip on her shoulder fell off. At five years of age, Geris reflected with a smile, it didn't take much.

Geris shrugged. *"Okay."* She thought about that for a moment, then scowled some more for good measure. *"But only if you hate Strawberry Shortcake. Me"* — she jabbed a finger toward herself — *"I like the Smurfs."*

Kyra's expression fell and Geris instantly realized she'd made a horrible mistake. When the girl started to stand up to miserably walk away, Geris felt, for the first time in months, panicked by the thought of being left behind. Her tiny hand flew out and tugged gently at Kyra's arm. *"I guess we can play both kinda dolls,"* she said quietly.

Light brown almond eyes clashed with wide silvery blue ones. Life would never be the same again.

"Okay," Kyra said, a small smile tugging at the corners of her mouth. She stood up and held out her hand. *"You wanna play hop-scotch right now?"* she asked as she pushed her glasses up the bridge of her nose with her other hand.

Geris smiled for the first time since her daddy'd died. Skinny mahogany fingers threaded through pudgy pale ones. *"You can jump first if you want to…"*

Rubbing her temples and forcing the old memories at bay, Geris reminded herself that there was only one way to stop the overwhelming panic she was currently feeling at the thought of having lost the only person in her life who'd ever mattered. And that one way was to find and collect Kyra.

Somewhere on the grounds of *The Smiling Faces and Peaceful Hearts Meditation Retreat* her best friend was walking around, most likely trying to find someone with medical training who could help Geris out of her faint. Yes, that sounded just like Kyra. She would have immediately gone for help.

Feeling better once she'd decided that Kyra was alive and well, Geris took one last steadying breath then turned on the heel of her fashionable jogging shoe to go retrieve her best friend. She even managed a faint smile and her heartbeat began to return to normal as she strolled away from the BMW.

"You see," she said in the way of self-assurance. "Everything's fine." She frowned, her lips pinching together in their trademark glower. She felt like an idiot for having believed her hallucination might be real for even a minute. "So quit muttering to your damn self," she muttered.

Her chin thrusting up, Geris walked briskly toward the exit doors of the parking facility, determined to get back to the camp as quickly as possible. She felt the panic begin to inexplicably bubble up again and forcibly quelled it. "Stop it, Geris," she quietly chastised herself. "Stop—*oomph.*"

Her words faltered as she unexpectedly stumbled to the ground, having tripped over an object she'd been in too much of a hurry to notice. She sucked in her breath and expelled it in a hiss as fire shot through her skinned up knee. "Shit!" she yelped, her hisses turning into small whimpers as she softly probed her knee. "Ouch."

Geris sat there on the hard concrete floor for a prolonged moment, then glanced around to search for the offending object. When she saw it, when her gaze landed on the very thing that had felled her, her eyes widened as bile churned in her belly. "Sweet Jesus," she breathed out, her chest heaving up and down as her heart began rapidly palpitating. "Oh Kyra—oh no."

It hadn't been a dream, she thought in horror as she held out a trembling hand and reached for her best friend's jogging shoe—a shoe that had been shredded into three separate pieces. The gigantic men, the glowing blue eyes, the possessive way the dark-haired one had stared at Kyra...

Geris swallowed roughly, convulsively.

"You wanna be best friends?"

Oh God oh God oh God oh God...

Light brown almond eyes clashed with wide silvery blue ones. Life would never be the same again.

Geris gasped as she clutched the shredded shoe to her chest and wept uncontrollably.

No. Life would never be the same again.

Chapter 1

Las Vegas, Nevada
Three earth years later...

King Dak Q'an Tal frowned down at Kita, not having a care for the two-arsed creature's insolent — not to mention noxious! — mirth. "The wearing of these odd leathers shall help me fit in here with the other humanoids whilst I find my onyx wench."

And he was certain she was his — oh aye was he certain. Due to mechanical troubles with the gastrolight cruiser, it had taken him longer than expected to get here but his cock had been nigh unto bursting with need since they'd broached the primitive galaxy they were now in. "Leastways, 'tis my hope," he mumbled as he absently adjusted his Elvis sideburns.

Dak sighed, not having a care for his attire any more than did Kita. And yet he had bore witness to many an admired male parading about the lit up city centre dressed thusly, singing to females who pawed at them as if in the throes of a sexual mating frenzy. And so Dak had relented and bartered with a tradesman for his new leathers, hopeful that Geris would find so many rhinestones and so much big hair appealing to her woman's senses.

Dak had been lonely for far too long, year after dreaded Yessat year passing in grim solitude with naught to distract him save the *Kefa* slaves and bound servants that paraded about the halls of the palace on Ti Q'won. His hearts felt empty, his life meaningless. There had to be more to it all than the warring arts and the development of weaponry that the green moon was renowned for.

He harrumphed. If 'twas bad hair and bad leathers that it took to woo his wench, then so be it. Leastways, he would change his leathers for a certainty once they boarded the gastrolight cruiser, he silently grumbled.

By the sands, 'twas a boggle what Earth women saw in males dressed thusly.

"I leave now to hunt, my friend," Dak said with growing excitement. The hellishly long trek had left him feeling a wee bit tired, aye, but he would waste not even a single Nuba-second in the hunting down of his *nee'ka*. Leastways, he frowned, the quicker he claimed her, the quicker he could change from these bedamned leathers and be gone from this hole of a planet.

They would need to return quickly, mayhap even launch through a time portal in deep space, for he'd already been gone far too long. Navigating at a speed fast enough to reverse time a wee bit would cost a hoard of credits in gastrolight fuel, but so be it. He had his sectors to see to and insurrectionists to bring to heel. Leastways, he couldn't think on that trivial matter just now. It all seemed trivial compared to the task before him, to the claiming of his *nee'ka*...

Dak ignored the foul odor Kita's laughing caused and patted his sideburns into place as he stalked from the rented chamber. He hoped that he had been right to take on the dress of King Elvis, for 'twould embarrass him to no end did Geris find him displeasing to look upon. He knew what his brothers (and mayhap others) thought of him, realized they believed him to be a warlord strong of the body, but lacking in wits...

His stomach knotted at the mere thought of Geris thinking upon him thusly. He wanted his Sacred Mate to love him, but a wench, he realized, could never love a warrior she considered to be lacking.

Dak blew out a breath, forcing the negative thoughts at bay. He consoled himself with the realization that it mattered not if his *nee'ka*-to-be believed him to be all brawn and no brains for 'twas to him and him alone that the fates had decreed her bound. For a certainty, that knowledge, the knowledge that she was his no matter her preference to the contrary, would have to do.

Aye, he sighed as he walked out into the neon-lit night. 'Twould have to do.

Chapter 2
California,
somewhere in the desert…

"Speak to us, Divine Mistress of the Light. Bless your child Geris Jackson in this her hour of need. Show us the—*nayyyyyyy!*—show us the way! *Nayyyyyyy…*"

Her mouth hanging open dumbly, Geris could only stare at the neighing Disciple Magda as the medium's eyes rolled back into her head until only the whites showed. Magda, the seventh—and final!—spiritual medium that Geris had hired in her three-year-old quest to find Kyra, was currently convulsing while she made obscene horsey sounds in the back of her throat.

At either side of the bald, robe-clad medium sat another bald, robe-clad disciple, both of them making various barnyard noises while they aided Magda in her communication with the Mistress of the Light. Disciple Helios was clucking like a chicken, his arms flailing like crazed wings at his sides, while Disciple Mercury brayed like a donkey as he did weird things with his tongue.

Geris's lips pinched together in a frown. Sweet Jesus in heaven.

Rubbing her temples, Geris mentally conceded that seeking out these people was probably the stupidest move she'd made yet. And as moves go, she thought on a sigh, she had made some rather dumb ones in the past few years.

Or desperate ones, depending upon one's vantage point.

At least this group of crazies was a safe, peaceable one, she told herself in the way of consolation. All of them needed to be locked up some place where they'd get regular injections of thorazine to be sure, but otherwise they were relatively harmless. A celibate cult, she knew she wouldn't have to fend off unwanted advances like she had from the leader of the last sect she'd traveled to. That leader had promised he could find Kyra, but had insisted the gods would only speak to him while having sex with Geris.

Uh huh. Yeah right.

"Speak to—*nayyyyy!*—speak to me—*nayyyy!*—Mistress of the Light!"

Cluck cluck cluck. Hee-haw hee-haw hee-haw. Nayyyyyy...

Geris shook her head and sighed, grimly wondering if her life could become any more pathetic. For three years she had scoured the globe, looking high and low for a woman she was beginning to fear had met a bad end...

No.

Kyra was still alive. She *knew* she was still alive. She just needed to think logically, needed to put the puzzle pieces together in a coherent fashion by herself, rather than relying on bizarre mediums and their mentally unstable followers to find Kyra. *Think girl*, she silently commanded herself. *Think...*

But she had tried the logical route for the entire first year of Kyra's disappearance, a nagging voice in her head reminded her. She had traveled to all of the Nordic countries where males were bred tall and broad, thinking it was a logical place to start looking since the men who had kidnapped her best friend were built so massively. But she had found nothing. She'd developed a taste for Scandinavian food and could speak broken Norwegian and Swedish, but that was the only thing that had resulted from her excursions into the northlands.

Think, girl. Think...

"Las Vegas."

Geris blinked. She hadn't realized Disciple Magda had come back down from the alleged spiritual realm. "Huh?"

"You'll find the answers your heart seeks in Las Vegas," Magda said cheerfully. Her bald head crinkled in tune with the corners of her eyes. "The spirit of the Sacred Horse showed me thusly."

"Oh." Geris didn't know what to say to that. She cleared her throat discreetly. "Did, uh, did this horse—"

"Sacred Horse," Magda interrupted in a worshipful tone.

Geris sighed. "...*Sacred* horse mention where exactly in Las Vegas I'd find Kyra?" *Arrg! As if this horse guy is real, Geris!*

Magda's bald head crinkled in thought. Geris watched her hesitantly, silently hoping the woman wouldn't start neighing again. There was only so much neighing a person could take in a day.

"As a matter of fact, the Excellent Spirit did tell me that." Magda's eyes had a faraway, dreamy, I-smoke-a-lot-of-dope quality to them. "The Sacred Horse is all-knowing in His Wisdom after all."

"Huh."

"Go to Caesar's Palace," Magda continued in a reverent tone that brought to mind Moses decreeing God's Will to the Israelites. "Within it you shall find the needs of your heart. The Excellent Spirit has declared it and so it is."

"Hmm." *Well isn't that a little too damn easy! I've been searching for Kyra for three years and now some horse is gonna hand her over just like that!* "Interesting."

"A skeptical heart," Magda said with her good-natured cheer undaunted, "is like an onion falling apart at the petals of desire."

Geris blinked. She could only assume that statement would have made sense if she was flying as high as Magda appeared to be. "Huh." Remembering her manners, as well as the fact that Magda and her followers had been nothing but hospitable to her since she'd found them a week ago, Geris smiled as she stood up. "I'd like to thank you for all of your help." *Not that I believe a word of it!* She nodded. "I'll be on the next flight to Las Vegas." *Yeah right!*

Magda's hand whipped out in a lightning-fast motion. She gripped one of Geris's hands in a show of strength that was a tad frightening. The baldheaded, robe-clad woman stared deeply into her eyes and in that moment Geris recognized an intelligence she hadn't seen there before. A cunning, a knowing...

She swallowed roughly, but made no move to pull away from the medium.

"The fair-haired giant has returned to this realm," Magda murmured. "If you wish to see your friend again, do not be a fool. Do as the Excellent Spirit has decreed."

Geris's eyes widened. She was too dumbstruck to speak. Magda knew about that...that...man? But how could she? How could she unless...

Sweet Jesus in heaven. This was getting weird.

"Okay," Geris breathed out, her heart beating rapidly. "I'll go."

And why shouldn't she? Geris asked herself. It wasn't as if she hadn't looked everywhere else on God's green earth for Kyra. What could a short plane hop to Vegas hurt?

"Very good," Magda said, releasing the grip she had on Geris's hand. Her eyes resumed their normal dazed state as if the eerie glimmer of knowing she'd shown but moments prior had never been. Her bald head crinkled good-naturedly. "Godspeed."

"Godspeed," Geris muttered. Good lord she needed a drink. "Thanks, uh, thanks for everything." She swallowed over the lump in her throat.

Magda nodded, appeased. "Remember, child, that upon every silver cloud a wily bird migrates."

Geris frowned. She didn't know what to say to that. But then, most people probably wouldn't know what to say to that. "Take care, Disciple Magda," she said sincerely. She hesitated, then smiled slightly as she flashed the medium the nanu-nanu sign from *Mork & Mindy* that the Disciples of the Mistress of the Light seemed partial to. They lived in a funky kind of time-warp. "And thanks again."

"Godspeed," Magda said a final time as Geris walked from the desert tent. "May your spiritual leaves fly high before the Spirit of the Bird shits upon them."

Geris nodded without turning back. At least that one she'd kind of understood. "Godspeed, Disciple Magda."

By the time Geris left the tent and reached the jeep she'd rented for this desert excursion, her legs were wobbly and shaking. "Good lord," she muttered to herself, her heartbeat racing. "How could that woman have known—"

The fair-haired giant has returned to this realm.

Geris's eyes widened. The fair-haired giant…

She gulped. She'd done her best not to think about him over the years because she knew in her heart it was the black-haired man who'd stolen Kyra, and therefore it went without saying that it was the black-haired man she needed to concentrate her energies on finding. But inevitably, perversely, her thoughts would always stray back to the blonde giant—the one who had studied her so possessively...

Geris rubbed her temples and sighed. Sweet Jesus, she needed a drink.

Chapter 3

"Well, here I am, Sacred Horse," Geris muttered to herself. "Now where the hell is Kyra?"

Geris handed the taxicab driver his fare and tip. She absently watched as a bellhop collected her bags, then paid neither the cabbie nor the overly cheerful bellhop any more attention as she walked up the steps leading to the white statuesque building known as Caesar's Palace. The elegant resort hotel was lit up festively tonight in preparation for tomorrow's heavyweight championship boxing bout, the lively décor promising patrons a taste of regality and decadence. Geris, however, was too consumed with her own thoughts to give it all more than a passing glance.

After checking in at the front desk, she walked briskly toward her suite, the cheerful bellhop in tow. "What are you in town for, ma'am?" the bellboy asked. He couldn't have been older than eighteen, she thought. "For the boxing bout?"

"Huh? Oh. Um—yes. For the boxing match."

"I wish I wasn't working tomorrow night so I could see it," he lamented. He even managed to complain cheerfully, she thought on a frown. "No such luck. I just hope they broadcast it on the wide screen TV in the lobby."

"One can but hope." She smiled. "What floor am I on?"

He glanced at the keycard. "Fourteen."

She nodded as they continued walking.

En route to the elevators, they steered passed a bunch of men dressed in hideously outdated wigs and clothing. Geris rightly assumed that an Elvis convention was in attendance at Caesar's Palace as well. Heavyweight champion boxers and fifty Elvises at the same hotel — only in Vegas, she thought with a small grin.

The men in costume were practicing their Elvis gyrations, a small group of women apparently lacking in taste packed around the throng and flirting their bleach-blonde heads off while the males crooned and patted their big hair. She shook her head and sighed, idly wondering how any female could aspire to becoming a groupie to men dressed like that. She would have been embarrassed to be seen with them.

Geris's forehead crinkled as her gaze strayed toward one of the Elvis impersonators, the one who was commanding the most female attention. Wearing an obscenely ugly white jumpsuit with flared bottoms and rhinestones plastered over every available inch of material, he stood taller than the other males around him by a solid foot and a half. The man's back was to her, but even without being able to see his face there was still something a bit too familiar about him...

She frowned. Sacred Horse indeed. She was well and truly losing it.

"Something wrong?" the bellhop asked.

"What? Oh... No," she said on a smile, turning her attention to the eighteen-year-old. "Nothing's wrong."

The bellboy shrugged, apparently unconvinced but not about to ask twice and sound like a nag. He had a tip to think of after all. "Elevator's here," he cheerfully announced.

She nodded, ignoring the burning sensation of déjà vu she was experiencing, ignoring too the feeling that someone or something was staring her down. As if. This entire trip was ludicrous. She would never find Kyra at Caesar's Palace. Never. If Kyra had made it this close to home, her tenacious best friend would have found a way to inform the police.

She had been an idiot to come here, Geris morosely conceded as she alighted into the elevator and turned around on her heel to face front. If anyone found out that she'd made a trip to Las Vegas based upon the delirious visions of a woman who had clearly dropped one hit of acid too many, she would look like an utter fool. A complete and utter fool.

The bizarre feeling of déjà vu grew...and worsened. Her eyes narrowed speculatively when the most intense and inexplicable feeling of being hunted swamped her senses. She felt the gaze of...something—or someone—penetrating her entire being. A possessive, almost primal gaze.

Geris glanced up just as the elevator doors began to close. Her heart thumped wildly in her chest and her eyes widened to the size of full moons as her gaze clashed with one Elvis impersonator in particular—

Her breathing hitched.

A giant of a man who was stalking towards her, his gaze piercing hers, making her feel funny inside. A giant of a man who threw off his black wig as he raced to beat the elevator doors, revealing long golden hair plaited at the temples.

A giant of a man with possessive, piercing, glowing blue eyes.

Oh. My. God.

Geris gasped as the gargantuan male came charging toward her. "What the hell?" she heard the bellboy mutter. Perspiration broke out onto her forehead as she willed the doors to close before the giant could reach her. *Oh god oh god oh god oh god…*

The doors hissed closed and the elevator lurched upwards. She whimpered in relief.

A spine-numbing roar of momentary defeat echoed up from the other side of the steel contraption. She could hear it from a floor up. In that moment she knew—*knew*—that he had come here for her. How he had known that she would be in this place defied logic and reason, but she was as certain of that fact as she was her own name.

"Who the hell was *that*?" the bellhop asked, gaping. "Should I call security on that guy?"

"Um…" She was so shocked she could barely think, let alone form a battle plan. "Yes," she breathed out, sanity returning. She needed him captured and questioned. She needed to get Kyra back. *Oh god— Kyra!*

Geris turned haunted almond eyes up to the bellboy. "That man is responsible for the disappearance of my best friend," she rasped out. Her heart was beating so rapidly she felt dizzy. "Call the police."

* * * * *

"Don't worry, Ms. Jackson, we'll find him. He couldn't have gone too far."

Geris half listened and half ignored the police officer on the other end of the phone's line as she briskly paced the floor of her suite. Las Vegas was a bustling city. Finding the giant could be mission impossible. Then again, he was large enough to warrant anyone's notice if he was lurking around out there. "Please let me know the second you hear anything. I'm staying at the hotel until he's located."

"Will do."

They said their goodbyes and she hung up the phone. With a sigh, she resumed her pacing. *Think, Geris. Think…*

The giant had come here for her. That much she was certain of. But why? Why would he want her to begin with? Did he know that she'd spent the last three years hunting him and his friend down? Did he mean to permanently silence her so no more questions would be asked? Was she getting that close to discovering the truth of where Kyra had been taken?

Her eyes widened as she swallowed past the lump in her throat. It was very possible that he'd come here to kill her. Very possible indeed.

Geris came to a stop, her pacing abruptly halted. She had two choices, she silently conceded. She could either sit back and wait for the police to catch this guy, which could be never, or she could go out and find him herself. Unfortunately, she thought grimly, both choices were potentially stupid.

If she waited on the police, he might never be found. If she, by some miracle, was able to locate his whereabouts herself, however, he might kill her before she could alert the police and have him apprehended.

Geris closed her eyes and took a deep breath. She had come close — so damn close…

Her eyes flew open and her nostrils flared.

There was no way in the hell she was backing down now.

Chapter 4

She felt like an idiot.

Dressed in jeans, a tee-shirt, a trench coat and black sunglasses, she supposed her attempt at looking inconspicuously undercover was probably about as effective as a tissue mopping up Tammy Faye Baker's face after a crying binge. "You look like a damn Nancy Drew wannabe," she muttered as she threaded through the crowds of downtown Las Vegas and back toward Caesar's Palace. "If you're lucky, maybe you'll meet up with one of the Hardy Boys."

One thing was for certain—she sure hadn't met up with the object of her obsession. She had looked for the giant in casinos, wedding chapels, stripper clubs, bars—even in churches. She'd searched in bakeries, delis, and two homeless shelters. *Nothing.* It was as if he'd once again managed to disappear off the face of the earth.

Geris's heart sank as it occurred to her that she might have lost her one and only chance at finding Kyra when she'd run off from the giant yesterday. If she'd not allowed those elevator doors to whistle shut in his face, she'd have her answers. She might be dead, but she'd have her answers.

Geris sighed when the entrance to Caesar's Palace loomed visibly in the distance. She was tired, so damned tired. Her feet were sore and her body ached. Every muscle she possessed was begging for rest. Knowing that there was a whirlpool tub to soak in when she finally reached her suite was the only thing keeping her moving at this point.

For the past eight hours she had hunted high and low, praying she'd find *him* just around the next corner. She never had. She was beginning to suspect she never would. At least not until he was ready to be found, if indeed that auspicious moment ever came to pass.

He was smart, she thought on a frown. Far too smart. Anybody that tall and broad who could manage to stay unseen while being hunted down by en entire police department was far too intelligent for comfort.

Geris's jaw clenched as she forced her weary body to keep moving. Just another few minutes and she could relax in the bathtub. The thought was akin to following a mirage in the desert—somewhat comforting, but seemingly too far out of reach.

Her thoughts turned to her best friend, to the one and only person she had always been able to count on in life. Remembering Kyra gave her strength, just like always. "I'll find you, sweetheart," she whispered to the wind. "Don't give up on me yet. I'm down but I'm not out."

Tomorrow, she silently vowed. Tonight she'd eat and rest up, but tomorrow she would find that giant if it was the last thing she ever did.

* * * * *

Geris groaned as she shakily stood up in the tub and reached for a towel. Her muscles felt like overcooked spaghetti noodles. She'd been relaxing in the hot waters of the lulling whirlpool for over an hour—probably not the smartest move she'd ever made considering that a whirlpool could make her sleepy on a normal day. Today was definitely not a normal day. Her overworked muscles had been put to the test, pushed to their limits. Relaxing them for over an hour in the bath had almost put her to sleep several times.

She climbed out of the tub and began patting her body dry. She was getting sleepier and sleepier as the seconds ticked by, but she knew that she needed to eat before she allowed herself to get some rest. She ran the towel over her breasts, over her long legs…

An eerie feeling of being watched, hunted, caused the tiny hairs at the nape of her neck to stand up. She stilled, the bizarre feeling as familiar as it was shocking. The sensation was, just as it always was, a stunning one. Very similar to the way a deer must feel when faced with unexpected headlights.

She was afraid to look up. So damn afraid…

"Ma'jiqo a feré, *nee'ka*."

The voice was deep—very, very deep—and strange. It sounded as though the man murmuring to her was speaking through a musical synthesizer. She swallowed—roughly—then slowly raised her head to look upon what she knew would be the giant.

Her breath caught in the back of her throat. It was *him*. Good lord in heaven—it was him! The same black leather outfit. No shirt. A bizarre necklace that pulsed in unnamable colors hanging around his neck. A necklace he was taking off...

"What do you want?" she breathed out. Her stomach knotted as she locked gazes with him. Good lord, he was huge. Even bigger this close up than he'd been at a distance. He was tall—at least seven feet and probably bigger. His musculature was extreme—heavy, defined, and vein-roped. Not the kind of guy you wanted to meet up with in a dark alley. Definitely not the kind of guy you wanted to find standing before you while alone and unprotected in your hotel room wearing nothing but a towel.

She frowned. He was also more handsome than she remembered him being. His face was perfect in its rugged, masculine beauty, his golden hair that hung to the middle of his back plaited off of his temples in a series of three braids. His skin was a tanned honey, his body as perfect as it was powerful.

How ironic, she thought glumly, that she had been fated to die at the hands of a golden devil with the face of a ruggedly masculine angel. "Where is Kyra? Where is she!"

He raised an eyebrow in such a way that she realized he didn't understand her words any more than she had understood his. She felt his eyes boring into her cleavage, and then lower, as the towel was pulled away from her body by forces unseen. Slowly. Seductively...

She gasped.

His glowing blue gaze wandered up and down her nude body as he steadily made his way towards her. Perspiration broke out on her forehead. Her heartbeat went into overdrive.

Run, idiot! Run and scream!

Her mouth worked up and down, but nothing came out. Her eyes widened as he grew alarmingly closer. She was able to gasp again when he reached toward her with his gargantuan hands, but that was all she seemed able to do. That necklace—*Help! He's going to strangle me with it!* Her heart was beating like a rock in her chest. *He's going to*—

The necklace clasped unforgivingly around her neck. She blinked, having expected something far more sinister. *What the...?*

Geris's wide, startled eyes flickered up to the giant's. "What do you want?" she whispered, at last able to speak. A strange calm stole over her, accompanied by acute fatigue. She did nothing, was able to offer no resistance, as two vein-roped arms reached down for her.

"You," the giant murmured as his hands grasped her waist and bodily pulled her up the long length of him. "Only you."

She was given no time to register that statement, let alone make sense of it. His mouth came down on hers—hard and unyielding, yet soft and gentle. His tongue thrust between her lips, forcing them open. Her eyes widened further, her mind telling her to fight him, but her body, for reasons unknown, unable to resist.

He palmed her buttocks as he kissed her, kneading them and squeezing them in his large, callused palms. He rocked her up and down, rubbing her clit against the erection bulging against his trousers. She whimpered, uncertain as to what she should do. Uncertain too as to why she still felt no fear.

He kissed her until she was breathless, until her hands were wrapping around his neck as though they were meant to be there. Until she'd forgotten that he was her enemy and that she hated him.

Until she was so tired that she passed out in his arms, dead to the world.

* * * * *

Geris awoke with a groan, her body feeling heavy as lead. Her eyes remained shut as she tried to think, tried to remember. Something wasn't right here. Something was very wrong...

The police, the giant hunting her down—

The way she'd kissed him.

Sweet Jesus, she was an idiot! What had she been thinking, kissing the very man she was certain had everything to do with Kyra's disappearance? The odd thing was she hadn't been thinking. It was like that man's bizarre gaze had sucked all rational thought out of her head until she'd responded to him like some sex-crazed simpleton.

Well no more, she thought, grimly. She would never...

Wait a minute! she told herself. Last night *had* to have been a dream. She was certain of it. Because no way would she have kissed that lunatic back. Uh-uh. Not in a million years. No sir—

"Good morn, *nee'ka*."

Well shit.

"'Tis wondrous to have you all to myself at long last," he murmured.

Sacred Horse, where are you when a woman needs you?

"Leastways, after we take Kita back to the planet from which he heralds, I will have you to myself anon."

He sure was chatty for a lunatic, Geris thought as her lips puckered into a frown. The man was talking to her as if they were lifelong best friends instead of bitter enemies.

"Where," she gritted out, getting right down to business, "is Kyra?" Her eyes flew open and clashed with the giant's. Her nostrils flared as she regarded him. Damn it! Why did he have to be so fine? It should have been a law that all lunatics had to be butt-ugly. "Where the hell is..."

She gasped, startled when she saw the second "face" hovering over the bed she'd been laid out—naked!—on. Sweet Jesus she was naked. Naked, and with a spotted guy who had a butt where his face should have been staring down at her, a beady little eye popping out of either cheek. She wanted to shield her body, but found to her dismay that the covers were quite a ways down the bed. She used her hands, as best as she could, instead. "What," she bit out, her words evenly spaced through clenched teeth, "is *that?*"

Sweet Jesus!

The giant ran a hand through her long hair, eyeing the micro-braids they were plaited in as though he'd never seen the likes of them. And as though they—and she—were the most beautiful things he'd ever gazed upon. She frowned again, wondering how it was that she knew what he was feeling. Wondering too why his feelings were making her heart thump in a strange way.

Who was the lunatic here? she thought grimly. Him or her?

"'Tis called a *pugmuff*," the giant said in an absent tone as his hands played with her hair, then softly trailed over her face. "We will take my friend home anon, then will we continue onward to Tryston that you might greet my brother and be reunited with my sister-within-the-law. From there we will venture onward to our home on Ti Q'won, the low-hanging green moon." He grinned. "Leastways, I will set you to hatching whilst there."

She blinked, not certain she was following the thread of the conversation. Also uncertain as to why she didn't feel overwhelmed with the need to get up and run. Huffing, she threw his hands off of her face.

"What in the hell are you talking about?" she shouted. "You don't make any damn sense!"

She could have sworn she saw him blush just before he glanced away. An act that left her feeling strangely...guilty. She'd hurt his feelings, she knew. She'd—

Huh? Arrg! She didn't even know him!

"What are you talking about?" she asked in a calmer tone of voice. She intensely disliked this urge she felt to shield the man's feelings, but there it was. "All I meant was that these words you are using—" She clamped a hand to her forehead and groaned. "I don't know what they mean...hey wait a minute!" She gasped. "We're not speaking in English!" Her eyes went a bit wild. "What in the name of God is going on here!"

"*Nee'ka...*"

Wife. He'd called her *wife*. Good lord in heaven! And just how did she know that he'd called her that?

"Where is Kyra?" she shouted as she jumped off of the extremely high bed and landed on her feet. She grabbed at the covers and pulled them around her. He frowned and snatched them off of her—without touching her!—somehow able to do it with his gaze alone. Just as he had done to the towel back in the hotel room before he'd stolen her away...

"Who are you? What have you done to my mind? Where have you taken me?" Her eyes went lunatic-frantic. "And what in the hell is that awful smell!"

She watched as the golden haired giant looked to the spotted little guy with the butt for a head and frowned. "'Tis Kita's mirth that causes the stench. And—"

"Arrg! I don't care, you idiot! Don't be stupid! I want—"

Geris stopped mid-tirade when she saw the giant's face fall at her words. She could feel his pain as if it was her own. Like a knife right through the heart and a punch directly to the gut.

"I'm sorry," she heard herself whisper. She blinked. Why was *she* comforting *him*? It should have been the other way around! She was the one who'd been without her best friend for three years and now found herself kidnapped by one of the men who had snatched Kyra so cruelly away. And yet she heard herself say, "I don't think you're stupid. It's just an expression that…"

He smiled.

Her words trailed off as she sank to the ground, her eyes wide and unblinking. "Sweet Jesus, what is going on?" she muttered. She wanted to cry. She'd never been more confused in her entire life. Tears that refused to fall gathered in her eyes as she looked up to the giant. "Please tell me what is going on."

* * * * *

An hour after Kita took his leave, and thirty minutes after Geris had ranted and raved at her captor about how she'd never fall for the explanations he'd given her, she stared dumbly at the gargantuan man who'd tried to sell her on a gargantuan-sized tale. It was a bit hard to swallow. Then again, everything about this situation was a bit hard to swallow.

"Let me see if I have this right," she grumbled. "Kyra—a tax accountant by the way!—is an empress. She is married to that black-haired dude that kidnapped her. Oh and he just so happens to be the emperor of this so called galaxy you herald from."

She harrumphed when he nodded. "You live in Trek Mi Q'an, which means, literally translated, *the galaxy of warriors*."

He nodded again.

Her teeth gnashed together. "More specifically, you live on the planet Tryston, a planet renowned in several dimensions"—her lips puckered as if she'd been sucking on lemons. Sweet Jesus, this man was as crazy as the medium Magda!—"for its healing sands and warriors."

"Aye, 'tis true your words."

She rubbed her temples and sighed. He still hadn't let her shield her nudity from him with the covers, which made her sigh all the more. "Can I ask you a question?"

"Aye, my hearts."

She frowned, not caring for what the sweet things he'd been insistently calling her by since her capture did to her stomach. Like make it pleasurably knot. What in the name of God was with that?

Sweet Jesus, this was nuts! All of it. From her bizarre reactions to him to the whopper of a tale he'd just told, everything felt insane. His story, if it could be believed, was as crazy as tall tales come:

A bridal necklace that made it possible for her to understand what was being said to her, and for him to understand what she was saying to him.

Sacred Mates—they had allegedly been decreed since birth "by the fates" to be married.

A best friend who was an empress.

A planet of warriors who ruled an entire galaxy.

An alien—she had been kidnapped and was to be forcibly married to an alien!

And yet…

She sighed. And yet in some bizarre way, it all made sense. She had not, in fact, been able to understand his words until that weird necklace cum translation device had been clasped about her neck. And that *pugmuff* creature—it was safe to say that anything with two butts was not from earth.

But if the story was true, then there was a piece of it that left her feeling decidedly dismal. "Why did Kyra wait so long to send you to come and get me?" She swallowed past the lump in her throat as she glanced away, her usual formidable exterior showing signs of vulnerability. "I mean, the Kyra I know would have missed me long before three years," she murmured.

It was her worst nightmare come to life. The best friend she'd searched the globe for hadn't wanted to be found. Had, in fact, abandoned her and their friendship for another life altogether.

"I know not your meaning." She glanced up in time to see the giant's—Dak's—forehead wrinkle. "Kyra did grant me passage to claim you immediately after her knowing period, the time she spent with my brother afore he resumed his duties."

Geris released a breath she hadn't realized she'd been holding in. "Oh." It was all she could think to say.

"'Tis different, your time from ours."

She tensed up when he came down on his knees and sat beside her, the muscles in his thighs flexing from underneath the black leather-like trousers he wore. He held out his hands and threaded them through her hair, gently massaging her scalp as he pulled her close against his chest.

She blinked. He was attempting to comfort her and she wasn't certain what she should feel about this show of caring. It was hard for her to trust others. It was impossible for her to trust someone she barely knew. Wasn't it?

What in the hell was he trying to do to her! He'd kidnapped her for goodness sake!

No matter how horribly she treated him—and she'd said quite a few nasty things after he'd first delivered his incredible tale—he still wanted to be near her. Most men would have given up after the first tongue-lashing. This one had survived three already and showed no signs of weakening or wanting to go away.

Since the age of five Geris had believed in no one and nothing except for Kyra, and of course, Kyra's younger sister Kara. Perhaps it was low self-esteem. Perhaps it was a fear of abandonment. Perhaps it was both. But for whatever reason, she had always felt as if there was something fundamentally unlovable about her. And now this man, this virtual stranger…this *alien*…was trying to make her feel things after a couple of hours in his presence that no man she'd dated had made her feel after months.

Like maybe there was something lovable about her after all. Like maybe the ice that was her heart wasn't as impenetrable as she'd thought.

Her spine went rigid when he brushed two micro-braids behind her ear.

"Our days are much longer than are yours, *nee'ka*. What was three years to you was more like three months to us. I vow to you that Kyra did want you back from the beginning. She detested being separated from you."

She closed her eyes at the caring in his voice. This was so overwhelming. It was too much to take in.

He tugged at her hands until they fell limply at her sides, no longer shielding her breasts from his touch. Her eyes flew open and widened on a gasp as his large, callused hands rested on her breasts, the thumbs gently stroking her nipples.

She raised her head from his chest. Their gazes clashed. She gulped.

"I have waited nigh unto forever to find you," Dak murmured. His glowing blue gaze did something strange to her insides, making her skin tingle a second before she was whisked by forces unseen from the floor of the room into his lap. She yelped, her arms instinctively flying around his neck. "Forever is finally here," he whispered.

Oh damn but he had a way with words. And what's worse, she thought nervously, was that she knew he felt exactly what he'd just said. She still didn't understand precisely how the bridal necklace she wore worked, but she was well aware of the fact that it was somehow able to convey his emotions to her.

His mouth came down on hers as though he couldn't help himself, his eyes closing at the same moment his tongue thrust between her lips. She whimpered, pushing at his solid chest, her mind wanting to fight him off but her body and her heart very much wanting to succumb.

He played with her naked body as he kissed her senseless, drugging kisses that had the effect of robbing her of what she had left of her wits. His hands toyed with her intimate places, exploring and surveying what she knew he considered to be his. She felt like a doll. Like a living, breathing doll the giant had found and would never give up.

It was unnervingly arousing.

He massaged her breasts and nipples, squeezed the soft, full globes of her ass, then went lower, teasing her pussy lips, his mouth working over hers the entire time, his tongue thrusting and retreating over and over again...

She gasped as his thumb began working her clit in small, firm circles. Geris's mind screamed to stop, but the longer she kissed him, the less resistant she felt towards him and his touch.

Breathing heavily, he tore his lips from hers and stood up. He whispered in her ear as he carried her toward the bed. "You are wet for me, *nee'ka*. Your body craves mine as much as mine craves yours."

Sweet Jesus. She wished she could say the man was lying.

She opened her eyes as she wet her lips, not bothering to deny the attraction she felt towards the golden-haired giant. He deposited her on the edge of the raised bed and forcibly spread her thighs apart. He didn't touch her for long moments, simply stared at her exposed flesh.

The effect was a heady one. Geris's breathing grew labored as arousal swamped all of her senses. Her dark nipples stabbed upward in reaction, jutting toward the ceiling. "Touch me," she heard herself murmur. "Touch my body."

Later she would deal with what she'd just done. Later she would tell herself how foolish she'd been to invite further intimacy with him. Later. Much, much later…

On a groan, Dak's face dove for her pussy, causing her head to limply fall back against the bedding. Her hips instinctually reared up as she ground her flesh into his face. He must have liked her reaction for inaudible growling sounds erupted from his throat as he feasted on her cunt.

"Oh goodness," Geris gasped, spreading her thighs impossibly wider. She couldn't open her eyes right now if her life depended upon it. He slurped her clit into his warm mouth, sucking on the swollen piece of flesh as his hands kneaded her thighs. *"Oh lord."*

His lips latched onto her clit like a kid sucking on a piece of candy, never letting go. She moaned gutturally, her hips rocking back and forth as if trying to mash her pussy against his face.

He sucked on her harder, and harder still. He growled into her cunt as he feverishly milked her clit, his lips and tongue working her body into a frenzy.

Harder. Harder still. Until she was bucking and writhing and moaning...

"I'm coming," she groaned, her eyes tightly closed as she listened to the arousing slurping sounds he was making. *"Oh god – I'm coming!"*

Geris came on a loud moan, her hips flaring up as her stiff nipples peaked impossibly further and harder. She climaxed so violently that she all but screamed, blood rushing to her face to heat it.

He purred against her cunt, still licking and sucking it as she gasped and moaned.

"Please!" she frantically begged. *"No more!"*

But Dak seemed to not hear her. Or if he did hear her, he paid her protests no attention at all.

He licked and sucked on her pussy for the better part of an hour, milking it of juice at least a half dozen times. By the time he finished, by the time he felt sated, she was so exhausted she immediately collapsed into a spent heap of flesh and bones, offering him no resistance when he laid her body out atop his gigantic one and fell fast asleep.

Geris sighed against his chest, simultaneously loving and hating how secure she felt lying against it.

* * * * *

For the next three days and nights Geris's body was touched in every sexual way but through actual penetration. Dak's hands were constantly on her, his tongue exploring places that made her blush. Her pussy, her anus—nothing was left unchartered. The mental comparison she'd made three nights ago about her body and a living doll turned out to be apropos. She felt like a walking, talking, sex doll.

And yet, nerve-wracking as it was, she felt like a very much loved and beloved sex doll. She didn't know what to make of it or how to react.

Geris put up a half-hearted protest every now and again when her alleged Sacred Mate began fondling her intimately, but she quickly tired of it. Her protests, after all, inevitably fell on deaf ears.

"I love you, my hearts," he would say. *"Do not shield your body from my lust."*

Not exactly a Hallmark card, but damn, repeated words like that were getting to her.

Dak touched her no matter where they were, no matter who they were in front of—his soldiers and the *pugmuff* included. He loved bringing her to what he called her "woman's joy"…so much in fact that she'd long ago lost count as to how many times she'd obtained it.

He seemed fascinated by her nipples and pussy, transfixed by everything from her micro-braids to the way her hips swished when she walked. Invariably, she always sat in his lap rather than anywhere else for he allowed her to do nothing else. It was as if he couldn't stand to be separated from her even the smallest bit.

And it wasn't just sexual communication either. If it had been, perhaps she would have been better able to shield her heart and emotions from the giant who claimed to be her destined mate. But it wasn't just sexual. They did a lot of talking too. Conversations about everything and nothing. Conversations about life on the green moon Ti Q'won and about how he'd been waiting for her all of his life.

Conversations that chipped away at the ice surrounding her heart like a goddamn pick ax.

Sacred Horse, what in the name of the Mistress of the Light have you done to me!

By the time they landed on planet Tojo, Kita's home world, Geris was more than ready to disembark. She needed a breathing spell, required some down time to think.

She was going insane. She had fallen in love with her nemesis in just three short days.

She frowned as they walked down the crystal steps that would spit them out onto the terrain of a large, orange-colored planet.

Who was she fooling? she nervously wondered. It hadn't been three days. It had been more like three minutes.

Geris sighed, conceding that if she didn't get some alone time, she was liable to go as nuts as she'd once thought the medium Magda had been.

Chapter 5

Geris's eyes widened as she stepped out onto a planet filled with buttheads…literally. She frowned, certain she'd never live to see a weirder sight. Spotted buttheads were everywhere she looked. Tall and short, thin and plump, old and young.

The beings of planet Tojo were possessed of orange bodies spotted with black markings. The bodies themselves were quite human looking in appearance, the only noticeable difference between them and earthlings their pumpkin coloring. Well that and the great big butts that were where their heads should have been.

Sweet Jesus, she thought on a sigh. What a day.

Geris absently accepted Dak's hand as they left the gastrolight cruiser and veered through the throng of citizens scattered about the chilly orange planet's main traveling port. She shivered, frowning when she recalled the obscene outfit she was wearing. It was hardly fitting for such a trip as this one. The wind was brisk, her nipples stiff from the chill, yet Dak had forced her to dress like a Penthouse Pet in a see-through blue number.

She gritted her teeth, remembering all too well how many hours they'd fought back and forth about her wearing what he called the *qi'ka*. The shirt, if one could indeed call it that, resembled a strapless genie top that cinched together in a knot between her breasts. The skirt, which looked like a pervert's wet dream come true, fell to her ankles and carried a slit all the way up her left thigh that ended at the hip. Like the top, it was cinched together into a knot, holding the flimsy garment together. The front of it fell below the navel, making her look sluttier than she didn't know what.

"'Tis the dress of my women," Dak had growled when she refused to wear it. *"You will don it and you will like it."* Three hours, several thousand heated words, and no choices left to her later, she had done just that.

Geris frowned. Sometimes the man could get on her last nerve.

"Damn baby, you look fine today."

Geris glanced up, her gaze landing a few feet away to where a male *pugmuff* was currently trying to hit on a female *pugmuff*. Dressed in leather, his back nonchalantly resting against a hovering vehicle that resembled a floating motorcycle, Geris tried not to laugh. But the entire courting scene looked like something out of a really bad fifties movie. The butthead version of James Dean trying to woo an innocent butthead virgin into his bed.

The female *pugmuff* he was attempted to court looked a bit shy. Naked except for a scarf around her waist, her long black hair was held away from her butthead face by a fifties looking headband made of silk.

Geris blinked when the male *pugmuff's* tongue lashed out, the two-foot long thing flicking down to taste the female's pussy.

"Mmm mm," the male purred in a series of clicks Geris somehow was able to understand—she supposed because of the bridal necklace but wasn't sure how. "That is one tasty cunt you've got, sweetheart."

The girl blushed. Geris's eyebrows rose.

"I bet you give great ass," he lecherously murmured.

Geris couldn't help it. She laughed. The girl glanced up and grinned back at her. Then she primly turned on her heel and began to walk away.

"You'll have to do better than that," the female threw over her shoulder to the embarrassed would-be suitor. "I've had better lickings from a Rustian."

Geris had no idea what a Rustian was, but she assumed it wasn't something the *pugmuff* wanted to be compared to. The butthead version of James Dean muttered something under his breath about haughty wenches needing to be brought down a peg, hopped on his floating motorcycle, and hightailed it away.

"We're here," Dak announced, looking down at Geris. He winked, a dimple popping out on his cheek. "This conveyance shall take us to Kita's family home. We will stay there mayhap one moon-rising then take our leave." His hand found her buttocks and squeezed. "I've the need to get you to Tryston anon," he said hoarsely, "that I might rut inside of you."

Geris frowned. Whether at herself for growing aroused at his perverted announcement or at him just because she couldn't say. "My heart be still. You have quite a way with words."

Dak's eyebrows wiggled. "I have quite a way with lots of things."

She harrumphed, ignoring his soft laughter.

* * * * *

"I refuse!" Geris spat out, her nostrils flaring as her hands flew determinedly to her hips.

"*Nee'ka*," Dak gritted. His jaw tightened and his nostrils did a little flaring of their own. "You have seen with your own eyes that the females of this world do not wear clothing save the sash of their tribe around their waists. You will remove the *qi'ka* and we will speak of this no more."

"Oh you're right that we won't speak of this," she fumed. "We won't need to because I refuse to walk around naked!" Her hand slashed through the air. "This stupid outfit you made me wear is bad enough!"

Dak sighed, pinching the bridge of his nose. "Geris…" he said reasonably.

"No."

"Geris," he ground out.

"Forget it."

"Ger-*is*," he wailed.

"I won't do it." She folded her arms under her breasts and pinched her lips together in a glower.

Five seconds later she shrieked when the clothing came off seemingly of its own volition.

*****

Geris was starving by the time they reached Kita's familial home, a colossal structure that resembled a coconut-shaped stone with two massive doors and windows scattered throughout five floors. She also realized that she didn't care much about her nudity because nobody even seemed to notice it. She refused to consider the possibility that the warriors her husband had brought along with them had noticed because she didn't think she could handle such a revelation at the moment.

And to think that they'd only disembarked less than an hour ago! Sweet Jesus—she could only imagine what other surprises lay in wait.

It was all too soon until she was to find out.

"Greetings unto you and your woman, King Q'an Tal." A regal looking blonde female *pugmuff* smiled sweetly. Geris rightly assumed that the female was Kita's wife. She exchanged kisses with Kita before turning back to Dak. "My sisters and I have prepared a bountiful feast in honor of your arrival. Please do my family the honor of joining us at table."

Dak waved his warriors away, telling them without words to remain outside and keep guard. He then turned back to Kita's wife and inclined his head. "The honor belongs to me and my *nee'ka*."

Geris frowned. She wished some gas masks belonged to him and his *nee'ka*. The smell of jovial *pugmuff* laughter grew worse and worse as they entered the large stone dwelling.

"Try to be nice," Dak said under his breath to her. "I know the stench is nigh unto vomit-inducing, but they are a good people."

"I wasn't born in a barn," she sniffed. Actually she had been born in a barn but that was beside the point. Her mama had been in the throes of labor when they'd been attending to grandaddy's horses while visiting him in rural Alabama. She'd ended up birthing Geris all alone out in the stables. It was a story she'd been told a few times. One that always made her smile. "Of course I won't be rude."

Dak clearly held his doubts, but he said nothing. He merely grunted as he took hold of her elbow and guided her toward where the feast was currently getting under way.

The males of the family, five in all, stood to greet the king and his queen as they strolled into the familial dining chamber. It was a crude, primitive looking room that resembled a jungle with a long table in the middle of it.

But at least it was warm. For the first time since they'd disembarked from the gastrolight cruiser, Geris wasn't freezing half to death.

"Welcome!" an elder male greeted. "Greetings to you both!"

Geris couldn't help but to smile. Dak had been right. The people here were, if not the best smelling creatures she'd ever encountered, certainly the friendliest.

The meal turned out to be a pleasant one, if a bit embarrassing. The males all gathered around a low table where they partook of foodstuffs together. The females sat naked on their knees, said knees spread far apart, their hands clasped behind their backs, while they were handfed by whichever male they belonged to.

Geris gasped when a two-foot long male *pugmuff* tongue landed on her pussy and began to lap at it. She bodily froze, her hands clasped behind her back, her knees spread wide apart, uncertain what she should do.

"'Tis all right," Dak whispered down to her. "'Tis how they greet a new bride here."

Oh of course! How could I not have known that! She sighed.

The tongue found her labial folds, softly swirling itself around the creases. She shivered.

The lapping, it seemed, was like a token of affection. Sort of like pets that lapped at your skin, she thought a bit nervously. Only these creatures were able to think at a cognitive level on par with her own.

Her eyes wide, Geris swallowed roughly. She didn't know what to do. On one hand she didn't want to offend anyone, but on the other hand this was just too much. The tongue that was softly lapping at her pussy was beginning to arouse her against her volition—a fact she didn't care for at all. But when she turned embarrassed eyes up to Dak, he didn't seem to think anything of it.

A second tongue joined the first, licking and caressing her vaginal folds.

Her breath came out in a rush.

A third tongue joined in, probing inside of her pussy hole.

She moaned, her eyes closing, her hands firmly clamped together behind her back.

A fourth tongue found her nipple and flicked at it. She shivered as it stiffened and elongated. The fifth and final tongue found the other one and snaked around it, hardening it.

"Oh shit," she said shakily.

The five tongues worked in concert, bringing her body to a fevered pitch in less than a minute. They lapped at her pussy, stroking in and out of it. They latched around her nipples and tweaked them frenziedly, making her instinctively writhe up and down on the tongue buried deep inside of her.

The tongue licking her clit picked up its pace, rapidly flicking at the piece of swollen flesh. She moaned, her head lulling back, her nipples stiffening impossibly further into hard points.

The tongues flicked and licked her nipples, sucked and explored her cunt. The tongue inside of her pussy hole felt like a vibrating massager, gliding in and out, in and out...

"Oh god." Geris came violently, groaning as her hips rocked back and forth. All five tongues darted down to her pussy hole, licking up the juice they'd managed to milk from her flesh.

When they were finished, the entire process repeated itself. The tongues didn't stop until Dak had finished hand-feeding Geris, some twenty minutes and four orgasms later.

By the time they were shown to their bedroom that night, Geris was completely spent. Dak merely chuckled as he came down on the soft pillows that had been laid out for their use and gathered her into his arms.

"'Twill be all right," he murmured, his expression growing serious. "I know this must be overwhelming to your woman's senses, all these new sights and experiences, but 'twill be all right."

She sighed, hoping that would be the case.

"Go to sleep, *nee'ka*. Fret no more." He bent his neck to kiss her softly on the lips. When she looked up, he was grinning. "But make sure you keep your legs spread. 'Tis the law here that a wench must sleep with her legs spread apart at all times."

She snorted at that. "Yeah right."

"'Tis true," he said seriously. "The Rustians of the planet feed on cunt juice. Much like the vines of Dementia or the male *yenni* of the fabled Khan-Gor. Without it they would soon expire."

Geris clamped a hand to her forehead. She had no idea what any of that diatribe meant so she latched on to what was closest at hand. "Back up a second. What the hell is a Rustian?"

"A lesser creature."

"A lesser creature?" She blinked. "You expect me to sleep with my legs spread open so if an animal finds its way into the room while we're asleep, he can feed off of me?"

He nodded. "Aye. 'Tis humane."

She frowned. "'Tis not happening." When he opened his mouth to protest, Geris clamped her palm over it to shush him. "Dak, forget it. Let's just go to sleep. If I'm a lawbreaker, oh well! We'll be gone tomorrow anyway."

He grunted, but relented. "Fine," he said as he removed her palm from his mouth. "But mayhap if one dies of starvation in the night you will feel guilt for a certainty—"

"I'll live with it," she muttered as she snuggled into her husband's side. "I think I've had enough alleged fun for one night. Let's just go to sleep."

* * * * *

Geris's eyes crossed as she laid there in the pillows, her husband snoring soundly beside her, two Rustians going down on her like starved pigs led to the trough. Sweet Jesus, she didn't think she could handle even one more orgasm!

A Rustian, it turned out, was a foot tall human-looking creature that was handsome as sin and dumber than a box of rocks. Dumb, but undeniably talented.

These creatures were wild and nomadic, making their homes were they would. Basically wherever they found a food source, which tonight at least, was between her thighs.

She didn't know how *pugmuff* women got any sleep at all with these forever-hungry Rustian things roaming around. They were gluttonous, eating like pigs, snorting into her cunt in a manner that left her gaping.

Geris whimpered when a third one ran over, his face immediately diving between her legs. Within minutes she had five of those little human things on her, sucking and sucking and...she groaned...oh good lord—*sucking*.

For the past four days it seemed as if all she had done was orgasm left and right, one climax after the other. Her brain had gone to mush she decided. That had to have been why she'd been relatively docile, at least for her, these past days.

She came again, shuddering as an orgasm stole over her. When the five Rustians were finished dining—what a concept!—she fell back onto the pillows exhausted.

She could only whimper when, not even a minute later, another wild pack of hungry little guys went diving under the covers.

Chapter 6

*Meanwhile, in the mining pits
on the green moon Ti Q'won...*

"In you go! The lot of you! Barot—get them in the bedamned tunnel anon!"

Barot hesitated. "They've had no food or drink for mayhap two days, sir. They might cause themselves an injury that—"

The mine-master narrowed his eyes at the overseer. "Did I ask your council?" he hissed.

The overseer swallowed roughly. "Nay. But—"

"Nay is the correct answer here!" The mine-master grabbed the younger male by the scruff of the neck. The crystal-gold arm bangle he wore tightened against the bulge of his bicep. His fetid breath wafted into the overseer's nostrils. "Mayhap you would like to trade places with one of the giant lackwits working the pits?"

"Nay, sir," Barot breathed out, his eyes wide. "I've a family to think of, sir."

"Then do as you are told." The mine-master shoved the overseer away from him. "We've ten moon-risings left to fill the king's order for crystal silius," he barked. "If I can't fill it he'll go to another mine for it." His nostrils flared. "Get those retards down there to move—anon!"

Barot inclined his head, then turned on his heel to see to the depraved task. He hated working the pits. More specifically, he hated working for Master Troz. Never had a viler male lived. Or a viler master. Had the bedamned Troz not squandered away the last reserve of crystal silius they'd located, he wouldn't be in a bind now to come up with fifty barrels of the stuff for the king's weaponry craftsmen.

But Troz had insisted the overtired and underfed workers proceed into the underground cavern the precious liquid gel had been found in and mine it straight through into the next moon-rising. One of the workers, exhausted and malnourished, had lost his balance and fallen into a pit of the boiling compound. During his horrific plummet downwards he crashed first into one of the delicate walls, causing the entire chamber to crumble and explode.

Such was how Troz had lost his last overseer and fifteen of his miners—not that the repugnant man had cared beyond the fact that the crystal silius had become unstable and had therefore been lost in the explosion with the retarded workers.

Leastways, it wasn't easy to find mine workers of crystal silius. Such a job was notoriously risky and associated with poor working conditions and early death. The liquid gel was highly unstable and given to exploding without notice. So mine-masters tended to acquire the workers in the most disgusting, irreprehensible manner imaginable—they bought them.

In a world where only the strongest of body and most cunning of mind prevailed, poor families were all too quick to unburden themselves of the males of their clan who were unlikely to succeed in the survival of the fittest. And so 'twas that mine-masters were quick to offer credits for the strongest of the dim-witted males, realizing as they did that they could work them to their deaths and nary a soul would care let alone report them to the high lords for the illegal goings-on.

Barot's jaw clenched as he strode toward the tired and hungry group of brawny, mentally dim workers. He would that he could cast Troz into a boiling pit of crystal silius himself rather than force twenty exhausted, malnourished men into the pits to mine.

He came to a stop before the assembled workers. A giant of a male named Myko, who was mayhap the most severely retarded of the workers, smiled fully at the overseer, his innocence so tangible as to be painful to the overseer. Barot guilty glanced away, hating his bedamned job. These men were mayhap dimwitted, yet still they were men.

He took a deep breath, blinking rapidly before turning back to the workers. Careful to keep his voice low, Barot said to them, "'Tis sorry I am to report that you shan't be fed and rested until the next moon-rising." When Myko only continued to smile, he sighed. "I fear that you must go back into the pits lest the master punish you more severely. All of you."

A seventeen-year-old male who rarely spoke worked his mouth up and down as though he was preparing to say something. The male was the largest of the entire crew, a giant standing close to eight feet in height and weighing several hundred pounds of solid muscle. He had survived the crystal silius pits for nigh unto ten Yessat years, a further testament to his incredible strength when most workers never lived past three. Barot knew that the seventeen-year-old had difficulty with speech, so he didn't push him to talk afore he was ready.

"I will g-go in M-Myko's s-staid," the seventeen-year-old giant said softly. "H-He is n-nigh unto ready to c-collapse."

Barot was given no time to reply for a ten-pronged whip lashed down on the giant's back just then, causing the seventeen-year-old to fall to the ground. The giant didn't protest the beating he was to receive at Troz's hands, having learned from past experience 'twas best to simply take it.

"You dare to tell me who will and will not work the mines, retard!" Troz spat out as the ten-pronged whip lashed down on the giant's back.

Barot winced. He closed his eyes briefly and said a prayer to the goddess as the whip lashed down a third time.

"I've no need of a dim-witted retard telling me how to master my own bedamned mines!"

The whip lashed down a fourth time. A fifth. Six. Seven. Eight…

The glow of the giant's eyes dimmed, indicating he was close to unconsciousness. His breathing was sporadic. Blood dripped from gaping wounds in his back. Yet still he did not whimper.

Barot's hand found his *zykif*. One more lash and Troz was a dead man. He cared not what the fates did to him at this point. He could stomach the sickening scene no longer.

Troz lifted his hand to strike a final time. Barot pulled out his *zykif* and aimed it at the back of his skull.

"I've grown tired of you and your dim-witted speech!" Troz bellowed as his arm rose in a strike meant to kill instead of maim. "I —"

The laser sound of a discharging *zykif* permeated the cavern, a sound that caused Barot's breath to intake for he had not fired yet. Troz's eyes widened as he fell to the ground, dead only seconds after he hit it. Barot spun around on his heel and came face to face with…

"Lord Q'an Ri," he murmured.

Jek Q'an Ri strode into the underground chamber, his pace brisk. "I came as soon as I received word. My sire is removed to Sand City, as am I for my training under the emperor's command, which is why it took so long to receive your summons."

Barot closed his eyes briefly, relieved. "Thank the goddess," he muttered. He opened his eyes and swiped the sweat at his brow. "I'm grateful you received it in time."

"As am I. But mayhap you should have informed the high lord of this sector rather than waiting on me."

"I didn't know who could be trusted, milord. Leastways, I knew I could trust you."

Given the trouble with insurrectionists ever afoot, Jek must have accepted that answer and realized the truth it held, for he said no more.

The high lord came down on his knee and examined the broken giant before him. His nostrils flared. "Have this male removed to the palace of Ti Q'won in posthaste. Since you are now master here, I also order you to have the other workers bathed, fed, and rested." His jaw clenched. "This is nigh unto disgusting! Do you mean to tell me this is usual for a crystal silius mine? Leastways, 'tis what you eluded at in your missive," he said without glancing back.

"I fear 'tis true," Barot sighed. "Never would I have believed such cruelty to be commonplace had I not seen it with my own eyes." He hesitated. "Mayhap I should send him to a healing dune. I shouldn't desire to inconvenience King Dak—"

"Never would my cousin think to turn him away." Jek gave his full attention back to the giant. He was fading in and out of consciousness, the seventeen-year-old's eyes as weak as his pulse. "I shall carry you myself," he murmured. "You require aid the soonest."

The giant stirred a bit, the high lord's words at last permeating. He was weak, Jek thought. Frighteningly close to death.

"I'm going to lift you up," Jek said quietly. "It will hurt. But I need you to keep your eyes open. Do not fade into the blackness again, my friend."

It took an extreme amount of energy to do it, but the giant managed to nod. His body was so broken and so bloody Barot worried the high lord would not be able to get him to help in time.

"What is your name?" Jek asked the giant as he prepared to lift him into his arms. "By what should I call you by?"

Barot knew the high lord was trying to keep the giant awake. Every time he slipped into unconsciousness he quickened toward death, toward the Rah.

The giant could barely open his eyes, yet from somewhere did he find the strength to do it. "My n-name is..." he said weakly, his voice a whisper.

"Aye?"

"Yar'at." His eyes found the high lord's. "My n-name is Yar'at."

Chapter 7

The next morning, Dak chuckled as he carried Geris back to the gastrolight cruiser. His poor wench was nigh unto exhausted, her wee body limp in his arms. "Are you well, *ty'ka*?" he asked on a grin. "Or have you the need of being brought to your woman's joy again?"

Geris's eyes, which had looked perpetually crossed since she'd awakened, rolled back into her head on a half whimper half groan. "Nyo nyooooo nyooomph."

A dimple popped out on his cheek. She kept mumbling incoherently when spoken to, sounding the frothing-mouthed lunatic, but otherwise spoke not a meaningful word.

'Twas mayhap best this way, he mused. For a certainty she tended toward the *heeka-beast* side whilst her wits were about her. He smiled fully, deciding to let his *nee'ka* sleep undisturbed when he got her into the gastrolight cruiser, for she'd need her energy in preparation for the joining.

Dak cradled her in his massive arms, both tenderly and possessively. 'Twas for a certainty he could not wait to remove himself to Tryston. Every moon-rising he laid beside Geris unable to join with her was more torturous than words could say. It took perseverance and strength of will he had never before had to exert. Leastways not in this fashion.

But soon, he thought, soon she would be all his. And then she wouldn't think to leave him again.

He knew the thought had to have crossed her mind a time or two, which hurt him more than he'd believed it possible for another being to injure him. Her emotions screamed for normalcy, for the desire to go back to all that she knew. It was mayhap only the hope of seeing Kyra again that kept her spirit in tact.

His nostrils flared. Nay. 'Twas not entirely true. He was fair certain that she was growing to have a care for him. Even if she'd never said the words to him. Leastways, he hoped that to be the case.

Because he was already in love with her.

In love with her in a way no male of her species could ever understand or come close to emulating. In love with her in a way that would cause him to literally die of grief if ever they were separated by the fates.

He could but hope that some day his bride would feel the same toward him.

It had been but five days. He allowed that she deserved a wee bit of time to settle into the way of things.

Dak sighed. He prayed to the goddess she would settle in quickly. If her woman's senses had been offended by the paltry goings-on of Tojo, he could but imagine the reaction she'd have to Tryston and its hedonistic ways.

* * * * *

"I cannot take any more surprises right now!" Geris wailed, stomping off to the other side of the bedchamber. "I am not—repeat *not*—leaving this ship again until we get to Kyra!"

"'Tis but a small duty I must see to!" Dak bellowed. His eyes narrowed into slits. "'Twill take but one moon-rising for me to hand deliver the missive to the lesser king and then we will set off for Sand City. You will see her in less than two days!"

"Dak," she said forlornly. Geris took a deep breath and glanced away. She could tell that he was tired of hearing about how much she wanted to get to Kyra. She supposed he wanted her to be eager to be with him instead. Good grief, what a situation.

Truth be told, she did enjoy his company. She enjoyed it so much that it frightened her. But the closeness had come too fast and too furiously to a woman who for all intent and purposes had once possessed ice where her heart should have been. At least where anyone except for Kyra and Kara were concerned.

Especially where men were concerned.

From a young age Geris had learned not to trust others, not to give them a chance to hurt her...or leave her. She didn't believe Dak would ever purposely do that—she truly didn't—yet she also didn't know how to explain to him that she needed some time in solitude to collect her thoughts and feelings.

The entire situation was overwhelming in the extreme. Having been brought to climax by her husband, five *pugmuffs*—sweet Jesus she'd never admit that to anyone!—and hoards of Rustians, only added to the feeling of panic quickly engulfing her. Good lord, her eyes had uncrossed only an hour ago!

Geris clamped a hand to her forehead and groaned. "I think I'm coming down with a fever."

Dak grunted. "Nay, wench. You are coming down with thoughts of bedeviling me is what you are coming down with. If you continue thusly," he sniffed, "'twill be grounded you are from your woman's joy."

Her lips pinched together in a glower. "That's not much of a threat considering that I've just now recovered from the last bout!"

He harrumped, ignoring that. "You will come with me, *pani*, and that is that." His massive arms crossed over his equally massive chest. "I will listen to your overtures no more."

"When do you ever listen to them?" she ground out, her chin thrusting up. Her teeth gritted further when she realized she was making eye contact with nothing but his abdomen. *Arrg!* She huffed as she backed up a step, then re-thrust her chin up so he could see the gesture. "I don't think you ever listen to them! In fact, I don't think you even give a damn about me and what I need! It's always about you!"

His nostrils flared. "You take this," he murmured, his words soft and even spaced, "too far."

"Oh do I?" she raged, irritated. "Do I really now, Your *Highness*" — she spat out the word like an epitaph. "I think the problem is that I've been in a daze this past week and therefore haven't had my wits about me to go far enough!"

Dak rolled his eyes. "*You* not go far enough. Now there is the bedamned day! I shall send missives to the four corners of the kingdom when at last it comes to pass!"

Her spine straightened indignantly. "I didn't want to take my clothes off on Tojo, but did you listen? Never!" Her nostrils flared to wicked proportions. "I didn't want those butthead people licking on me either, but did you care? Of course not!" Her jaw clenched. "I didn't want those Rustians treating my body like the drive-thru window at McDonalds, but did you stop them? Never! I think that—"

"Silence!" he roared, his hand slashing through the air. "Queen or no, you could have been arrested and jailed for wearing clothing on Tojo! And I told you already about how they greet new brides!"

"I don't like your world," Geris hissed, her eyes narrowing. "And I refuse to go anywhere else with you except to Kyra."

She felt a tremor of sadness pass through him, but steeled herself against it. She would not be swayed. Not for any reason. Enough was enough and her limits had definitely been reached and surpassed days ago.

"Geris…"

"No," she said firmly, her gaze locking with his. "You go. I am staying here where nothing new is going to pop out at me." She frowned. "Or decide to make a meal of me."

His jaw tightened.

"My mind," she said softly, "is not changing. If you take me, it will be kicking and screaming the entire time."

"I am left with no choice but to deliver this missive," he ground out, his jugular bulging. "Which means you must accompany me into the sector."

"No."

He sighed as he absently ran a hand through his golden blonde hair. "*Nee'ka*, the trek will last mayhap several hours. I shan't return until the next moon-rising. 'Tis for a certainty you must accompany me."

"No," she said quietly, but in a tone that broached no argument. "You go on without me, Dak. I want to be alone tonight."

His body stilled. "I see," he whispered.

Geris flinched as if she'd been physically lashed out at. Damn it! She didn't want to hurt him but she really needed some time alone. She straightened her shoulders and made eye contact once more. "I'm going back to bed now. You go do what you need to do. I'm staying here."

Dak looked away. He was quiet for a long moment, but finally relented with a nod. "If being without me is what makes you content then I shall endeavor to make myself scarce more oft."

Geris closed her eyes briefly, sighing as her husband walked away.

* * * * *

The next two days and nights would prove to be the longest, and loneliest, of Geris's life. They would also prove to be the guiltiest. She knew Dak was pining away for her, knew too he was feeling hurt by the perceived rejection. It only added to her already gloomy mood.

She even missed her "woman's joy", damn it! Her teeth gnashed together as she admitted that Dak's punishment was working. She missed the way he touched her, the way he held her…

She sighed. She missed everything.

A week ago when Dak had explained to her about how life worked in Trek Mi Q'an, about Sacred Mates and the like, she hadn't precisely believed every word he'd uttered as though it was the gospel truth. It seemed a bit strange to think that a prolonged physical separation could make a person so depressed that they couldn't sleep or eat. Yet that is exactly what had happened to her.

If Geris had to recount how she was feeling to a fellow earthling, she wasn't convinced that she could explain the sensations in a way that would make sense. It was like taking the blackest, most grueling day of your life and magnifying it a hundredfold. It was more painful than words could express—both physically and emotionally.

Dak had said it was very possible for Sacred Mates to be separated while traveling or what have you without experiencing the accompanying darkness. But it required the ingestion of a special healing sand or incantations being offered up by a priestess. Neither of which they had been given.

When Sacred Mates find each other, he had said, it's like two halves of a whole locking and fusing. Trying to break those halves up again, for any reason, causes death to both parts of the whole. The only way those halves can successfully split for a time, and even then it can only be done for brief spells, requires steps neither of them had taken. Had Geris known she was to spend these two days and nights feeling so depressed she could barely breathe, she would have thought twice about her insistence at staying behind.

She gritted her teeth from where she laid alone in the huge bed. Perhaps he had stayed away two nights instead of one to teach her this lesson. An effective punishment considering that she missed him so damn much.

Ooooh he was good! she seethed. A worthy opponent, but one who was too smart for comfort. Her only consolation was realizing that Dak was feeling as distraught and depressed as she was right now. If such could indeed be termed consolation.

For she also carried the added burden of knowing she was the one who had made him feel that way when all he had wanted was to be near her.

Chapter 8

By the time Dak returned on the third day, Geris had herself worked up into a bubbling cauldron of confused, ready to explode, emotions. She knew that she loved her husband, knew too that she'd missed him so much it had damn near killed her, but her pride wouldn't let her dash into his arms like some pathetic, weak-willed female greeting a returning hero.

Dak had, perhaps, given her too much time alone to think.

One of her biggest worries was that his promise to take her to see Kyra had all been a big ruse and she would never see her again. It was the hope of being reunited with her best friend that had kept her from offering Dak too much resistance when he'd first taken her.

It was the fact that she had fallen in love with him that kept her from resisting after that.

She hated to admit it, but she was feeling forlorn as hell. Not just about Kyra either, but mostly about the bizarre, way too distraught reaction she'd had when Dak had been gone these past three days.

It wasn't natural—not to a human woman. And anything unnatural felt blood-curdling frightening.

The worst of it was, she thought with a fallen heart, he hadn't even bothered to come to their room right away and inform her of his return. Instead, one of his warriors had seen to the task, telling her to be prepared to land in Sand City in an hour. She would have thought that Dak would be as desperate to see her as she was to see him. Considering the possibility that he wasn't even close to the same level of despair didn't bear dwelling upon.

Pacing briskly, Geris didn't know whether she should feel relief or anger when she heard the door to the room whoosh open and saw her so-called husband stroll in. He looked tired—very tired. And about as down in the dumps as she felt. But if that was the case, then why hadn't he come back to her sooner?

She kept pacing, her nostrils flaring. She refused to show him her weakness.

"Greetings, *nee'ka*."

She said nothing.

"I said—" He sighed. "What does it matter?" he muttered.

Geris stopped pacing and turned toward him. Her eyes widened a bit. He looked even worse than she'd thought on first glance. Simply awful. His long, golden hair hung limply around a face that could best be described as haggard. His blue eyes were drawn at the corners and bloodshot, as though he hadn't slept a wink.

Yet still, she thought on a defeated sigh, he was the most handsome man she'd ever laid eyes on. She loved him so much it was a tangible thing, as if she could cut her feelings with a knife. Not that she was anywhere near ready to admit it out loud.

Her back went rigid. Her chin thrust up. It didn't matter. She was the Rock of Gibraltar. Unbendable. Unbreakable. She would not and could not be swayed.

"Did you miss me?" he asked hoarsely. "Because I missed you so much it hurt."

Well, shit…

Geris frowned. "Of course I missed you!" she huffed. So much for not swaying, she thought grimly. "I can't believe you stayed away that long!" she shouted. "You had to have known what it was I'd be back here going through!" She clamped a hand to her forehead and groaned. "You've put a curse on me or something," she mumbled. "I always have this instinctive need to be near you. And worse yet to be nice to you."

"Really?" he asked quietly.

She looked up in time to see his glowing blue eyes sparkling in a way that made her feel happier than she wished it did. She frowned severely.

"Mayhap 'tis the same malady I too have been struck with." He grinned, that damn, fine as all hell dimple denting his cheek. "Yet I rather like this malady. 'Tis better for a certainty than what happens to my stomach after partaking of spoiled *matpow*."

She tried not to smile.

His expression turned serious. He reached down to her, threading his calloused hands through her micro-braids. "'Tis sorry I am that I stayed away so long," he said softly. "I meant to teach you a lesson, I do not deny it, yet I never planned to stay away for two moon-risings. There were political troubles afoot that I could not, in good conscience, turn my back on."

Geris closed her eyes when he pulled her against the solid warmth of his chest. She breathed deeply, feeling her first peaceful moment in days. "Thank you," she murmured. "For telling me that. I was afraid that..."

"That what?" he prodded when she didn't continue.

She sighed, hesitating for a moment. "That you didn't miss me as much as I missed you."

"Ah, *nee'ka*, do not ever think thusly." He held her closer. "'Tis goddess' truth I missed you so much my bedamned eyes almost had a tearing fit." He grunted. "'Twas a sorry sight when trying to keep two lesser kings from battling."

She grinned against his chest. They stayed there together like that, neither of them speaking, for a long pause.

"Are you okay?" Dak asked, his tone gentle.

Geris sighed, breaking away from him. "Truthfully?" she asked as she stepped back and made eye contact.

"Aye."

She shook her head. "No. No, I'm not."

His forehead wrinkled but he said nothing.

"It's just..." She took a deep breath. "I'm confused. I mean, really, really confused. This 'malady' as you call it might be normal to you, but it's freaking me the hell out."

Dak ran a hand over his jaw, uncertain as to what he should say. This eve they would be joined. Once they were she would be fine. But if he said as much she'd put questions to him that he didn't know how to answer. Such as why the joining would make everything all right. He didn't know why. He only knew that it was so.

"Let us not think on it just now, *ty'ka*," he hedged. "All will be well."

She seemed to think that over for a minute, but finally relented with a nod. "Fair enough. I know we have to disembark again right now anyway." She frowned, a thought occurring to her. "Just tell me something."

One of his eyebrows rose. "Aye?"

"You don't have any of those Rustian things in Sand City do you?"

He smiled. "Nay."

"And no buttheads that go licking anything they want to?"

"Nay."

She grunted, momentarily appeased. "And you swear you won't ever tell anyone about what those *pugmuffs* did to me?" Sweet Jesus, she'd die of embarrassment!

"'Tis a vow amongst Sacred Mates." He grinned. "Unless you think to bedevil me again in which case I

84

will send out missives to the four corners of the kingdom."

She frowned. "And no more grounding me from my woman's joy." She harrumphed at his triumphant look for she'd just all but admitted to the fact that not being touched by him felt like a death sentence. "A woman," she sniffed, "is entitled to her damn joy."

* * * * *

Oooooh he was a dead man! Geris seethed, her eyes narrowing. This was it. The straw that broke the camel's back. And to think she'd been so upset when they'd been apart for the past three days!

The minute they strolled through the palace doors, and an impressive palace it was, she begrudgingly admitted, she could only gawk. The first sight that greeted them in the black crystal structure was that of three naked female slaves—what her husband had called *Kefa* slaves—walking stoically into what she was told was a communal bathing chamber. The females were various shades of blue, all of them possessing a sparkly skin tone. As she and Dak continued down the corridor, she saw the slaves join a blonde warrior, all three of them sexually attending to the singular male.

Slaves, she thought dismally. Dak had mentioned as they'd walked passed the bathing chamber that he owned hundreds of them. How in the name of God could she live with a slaveholder?

From there it only got worse, for Geris was to get a rough idea for what a bound servant was. Basically, she thought in horror, it looked as though they were yet another type of sex toy for warriors to use as they would. She was beginning to get the heartbreaking picture that the males of Trek Mi Q'an were not a monogamous species. The most depressing thought imaginable to her way of thinking. She knew she could never be happy sharing her husband with other women.

The very moment they entered what Dak called the great hall, two of those topless bound servants ran up to him, their breasts bouncing as they giggled, rubbing their hands over his belly and crotch. "We've missed you!" one said excitedly. "Our channels hunger for the feel of you," the other one purred.

That did it.

Her nostrils flaring, Geris made a horrific gurgling sound in the back of her throat. She raised her hand to—she didn't know what she'd do—but it didn't matter anyway for she changed her mind and decided to leave as fast as her feet could carry her.

Turning on her heel, she made to run from the great hall. She didn't care what she had to do to escape, but escape she would. So far she hadn't seen Kyra, she found out she had a philandering husband, and there were naked slaves everywhere. Sweet Jesus! This was just too much!

Unfortunately, she had to pass by Dak and the two bimbos in order to make good on her escape. She was too angry to let that deter her. She was nimble, she knew. Nimble, fast, and agile. She would escape him. She would thwart him. She would—

A vein-roped hand firmly snatched her back, allowing her to go no further.

Well, shit…

Dak, who was trying to set the bound servants away from him, frowned as his arm snaked out and wrapped around her middle. "*Nee'ka*, where do you think to go?"

"Away from you!" she hissed, her eyes narrowed. She struggled, trying to free herself of his hold. "Let me go," she gritted out.

"Nay, I will not." His forehead wrinkled. "What ails you?"

"What ails—Dak! I can't stay here. I can't be here." She felt like she was going to vomit. Worse yet, her recently thawed out heart felt like it was being ripped into two. "We've been in this horrid palace all of twenty minutes and already I can tell that I need to go back home! You go to those…those…women of yours," she spat out, "and leave me the hell alone!"

His jaw tightened. He firmly set the two bound servants aside with his free hand and carried a kicking Geris over to the raised table to speak privately. "Enough," he said firmly, restraining her kicking feet. "I said enough!" he bellowed. "'Twill be put o'er my knee you are do you keep up this nonsense!"

"Put over your—Ooooo!"

His eyes narrowed. "You are having a fit of temper o'er naught. Cease this! I am sticking my staff in no wench's channel but yours."

"You're a real Shakespeare," she ground out. "Now put me down!"

"Not until you cease this nonsense!" He sniffed. "Leastways, not until you believe me."

"Well I don't," she seethed, still struggling to break away. "And what's more I never will. This place is awful. I already hate it!"

His nostrils flared. "Cease this anon!" he bellowed. "Your bedamned shouting gives my head the ache!"

"Then let me go!"

"Nay. Now cease! 'Tis an order I give to you."

She'd never know where she found the strength to do it, but she managed to break away from her infuriating husband. Jumping up on the raised table, her eyes darted madly about as she tried to figure out her next move before she was recaptured. *Think, girl. Think...*

"Ger-*is*!"

She gritted her teeth, realizing she'd never be able to get by him to go through the door. Infuriated, angry, and feeling as trapped as a wild animal, she warbled out a cry from the depths of her throat, picked up a bottle of that *matpow* junk Dak was partial to, and held it above her head like a weapon. Bound servants scurried to the other side of the table, their jaws dropped open, not certain what to do.

Geris's eyes locked with Dak's. Her jaw tightened. Without glancing away from him she said to one of the bound servants, "Go give a message to your leader from me. And here is what I have to say…"

* * * * *

Kyra, Zor, and Kil entered the great hall in time to witness Queen Geris having a royal fit of temper. She was standing on top of the raised table, preparing to throw an extremely expensive bottle of vintage *matpow* to the ground. Her bridal necklace was glowing an ominous red, indicating that her husband was pissed.

"Ger-*is*," Dak reprimanded in his most chastising tone, "you will put my brother's bottle of *matpow* down anon, else will you be grounded from your woman's joy for a full sennight after the joining." He crossed his arms over his chest and frowned formidably.

Kyra was amused to note that her best friend actually hesitated. Then, scowling, Geris hoisted the bottle higher into the air, preparing to render it to shards.

"Please don't," Kyra grinned, making her presence known, "that happens to be my favorite label."

Stunned, Geris whirled around. She could scarcely credit what it was, or who it was, that was standing before her. "Kyra?" she asked quietly, disbelieving what she was seeing.

"Ger?" Kyra took a step forward.

"Kyra!" Geris beamed, smiling from ear to ear.

"Ger!"

Geris's heart felt as though it might beat out of her chest. For three years she had hunted high and low for her best friend. For three long, goddamn years...

The two women squealed, running toward each other at top speed. When they met, they danced around in a circle, hugging and laughing. Dak grabbed the bottle of *matpow* out of his recalcitrant wife's hand while she was distracted.

"Kyra!" Geris laughed, running her hand down the side of her best friend's face to make certain she was really there. "It *is* you, girl!"

"And it's you!" Kyra beamed, tears streaming down her face. "I missed you so much!"

The two women chattered nonstop, taking seats by the raised table. They couldn't seem to stop hugging...or crying.

"I searched everywhere for you," Geris whispered. "Quit my job and everything."

"Oh Ger..."

"I was beginning to fear you were dead, Kyra. My God—" She closed her eyes and took a deep breath.

"Oh sweetheart. Oh Ger." Kyra threw her arms around Geris's neck and hugged her tightly. "You know I'd never leave you. Even if you hadn't belonged to Dak I would have figured out a way to get word to you about what had happened to me. And I would have prayed you would choose to come here and be with me."

Geris raised her head. She snorted. "Lord only knows if the man who took you is as bad as Dak, he will never willingly let you go. I guess coming here would have been my only option."

Kyra sighed. "Zor can be such a jerk, but I do love him." She searched Geris's eyes. "But I love you too. So much so I couldn't bear being separated from you."

"I love you too," Geris sniffed. "My God, we sound pathetic!" she laughed. She had never been comfortable with displays of emotion. A fact Kyra understood, shared, and respected.

"Hey," Kyra said softly, "we have pathetic coming to us." She smiled. "Now shut up already and hug me again. Hug me like you're never gonna let go."

Geris did. And damn if it didn't feel so good she started crying again. They were silent for a long while. They simply embraced, both of them overcome with emotion, neither of them ready to speak.

When they at last broke apart, Geris blew out a breath. "I don't know how you put up with this place, girl. I have to admit that if you hadn't showed up when you did...well, let's just say that I was feeling angry and depressed enough to escape—or die trying."

Kyra's forehead wrinkled. "Why? What happened?"

Geris told her about the slaves and about the bound servants who had rubbed their bodies along Dak's. "It was horrid to watch. I felt like I was going to be sick."

"You don't have to worry about them. I promise. After the Consummation Feast tonight..."

Geris's eyebrows rose. "Wait a second. Consummation Feast?"

Kyra glanced around, a bit nervously to Geris's way of thinking. She narrowed her eyes as her best friend nibbled at her bottom lip.

"Dak, uh, didn't tell you about it?"

"No. This is the first time I've ever even heard it mentioned. What the hell is a Consummation Feast?" Geris sighed. She rubbed her temples. "I really don't think I can take any more surprises. I've had more than my fair share these days," she said grimly.

"Hmm..."

Geris met her gaze. "Come on, Kyra. Tell me what's going on."

Kyra sighed. "You said you didn't want any more surprises."

"Oh shit. That sounds ominous. Just get it over with and tell—"

"Here comes Ari," Kyra breathed out.

It made Geris decidedly nervous that her best friend was holding back on her. "Kyra, what—"

"Ari is the Chief Priestess here," Kyra said a bit too quickly. "She'll answer all of your questions. If you have more when she's done counseling you then put them to me, okay?"

Geris stilled. "I know you. Better than anybody. What is going on?" she bit out.

Kyra's mouth worked up and down, but nothing came out. Before she could say anything more on the subject, one of the most stunningly beautiful women Geris had ever seen came strolling up to where they were seated. Geris blinked. A second ago the woman had been clear across the hall. A second later she was standing before her. What the hell...?

The gorgeous blonde-haired woman smiled. She inclined her head. "I am called Ari, Your Highness."

Geris looked around, wondering who the lady was talking to. "Oh! You mean me." She sighed. "I'm not used to people calling me that," she muttered.

Ari grinned. "'Tis all right." She held out a hand. "If you would come with me anon, I will instruct you on life in Trek Mi Q'an."

Geris's eyebrows shot up. "I could have used you a week ago."

Ari said nothing, only smiled. "Come. We shall partake of the ceremonial bath together."

Geris bit her lip. She glanced at Kyra who was purposely avoiding her gaze. Her eyes narrowed. "Ooookay," she said cautiously, turning back to Ari. "I'd like to hear what you have to say."

Chapter 9

Sweet Jesus.

Those two words would swim through Geris's mind more times than she could keep track of during the course of the evening. She had thought the experience at the mouths of the Rustians of Tojo was bad enough. The *pugmuff* experience had been a bit worse as far as humiliation is concerned. Being manhandled by Dak whether asleep or awake, *Kefa* slaves, bound servants, climaxing with a priestess in the bathing chamber "whilst they talked" —

Sweet Jesus! Sweet Jesus! Sweet Jesus!

It had all been enough to make a woman made of lesser stuff swoon. Geris was not made of lesser stuff and yet she still felt like swooning. All of those experiences were overwhelming singularly speaking, but when you put them together and then added them in with this Consummation Feast...

"Bastard!" Geris snapped, jumping to her feet. "Two-timing dog!"

Dak paled, grimacing even as he climaxed. "'Tis naught but tradition, my hearts!" he called out on a moan from across the great hall.

"Tradition my ass!" Geris screamed, her eyes smoldering him where he sat. "Get that blue bitch off you now!"

Kyra and another woman called Tia pulled her back down in her seat. "'Twill be all right," Tia informed her soothingly. "Kyra did have much the same reaction, though one not quite so loud." At Geris's frown, Tia hastened to add, "you will get your revenge the soonest."

"Oh really?" Geris scowled, crossing her arms under her breasts. "How?"

Kyra and Tia looked at each other and then at Geris, giggled and simultaneously informed her, "you'll see."

She felt like she was in a daze. All Geris could do was stare at what was going on around her and try not to lose it. And this was how they greeted new brides? By forcing them to watch as *Kefa* slaves sucked their husbands off? Good grief! She'd hate to see how these people greeted enemies!

"It better be true," Geris said under her breath to Kyra. Her jaw clenched. "Those slaves better not be real women."

"They aren't, Ger," Kyra whispered. "I swear it. They are like dolls. Or 3-dimensional virtual reality games. They have no thinking processes. They aren't even real."

But it didn't matter to Geris. The longer she watched, the angrier she got. By the time the women's turn rolled around and Geris was splayed out on a raised table while a handful of unmated warriors brought her to climax, she was so mad and hurt that she felt like smacking Dak across the face.

Not that it would have mattered to him, she thought glumly. She was learning quickly that in this galaxy of warriors the men had firm notions on how things were to be done, notions that had been firmly ingrained after billions of years of evolution and ritual, and not one of them was keen on changing the status quo.

Her nostrils flared as she spread her legs as far apart as they would go, giving the unmated warriors gathered around her easy access to any part of her body they wished to touch. If Dak wanted ritual, then she'd give him goddamned ritual…

Geris's eyebrows rose when she realized that Dak was pissed. Huh. So he didn't like it when these other warriors touched her. Apparently the *pugmuffs* and Rustians had been below his notice, almost like vibrators, but the warriors were a different story entirely.

Good! Good! Good!

Seething, her nostrils flared as she turned to regard Jek. "Is that the best you can do between my legs? A friend of mine back on earth named Dot used to sell vibrators that packed more power!"

Jek smiled slowly, fully aware of the fact she was trying to egg him on in an effort to make Dak jealous. "Is that a challenge you have issued me, my queen?" he asked softly.

Geris bit her lip, uncertain if she'd gone too far. "Um...well..."

His face dove between her legs. Her eyes crossed as her head fell back against the table. "Oh yes that was a challenge. Good lord above, I am definitely challenging you."

"Naughty wench," he murmured from around her clit. "You need to be taught a lesson."

Geris gasped as Jek sucked her clit into his mouth. She moaned when another warrior's mouth clamped around one of her nipples. Her hips bucked up when a third warrior's tongue snaked around her other nipple. "Shit," she breathed out. "Oh my god."

They sucked on her body for long minutes, bringing it and her to a fever pitch. Jek made appreciative *mmm* sounds as he sucked on her cunt, the sound of him slurping her flesh into his mouth as arousing as what his mouth was doing to her. Warriors sucked on her nipples, more warriors massaged her legs and feet. Other warriors began to gather around, two of them kissing and tonguing her belly and navel...

"Oh my god!"

Geris screamed as she came, hot blood rushing up to her face and heating it. Her nipples stabbed upwards, giving the warriors at her breasts more to suck on.

She wasn't given any time to come down from the climactic high, for a moment later she heard Dak bellowing at the warriors who had made her come.

"Do not touch her again!" he snarled. "Move away anon lest I have you sent to the gulch pits!"

The next thing Geris knew she was being hoisted up into the arms of a very angry, very jealous, and very aroused male who outweighed her by two hundred and some odd pounds. She bit her lip, a little leery. Perversely, however, she was also enjoying this display of extreme emotion. Especially given the fact that she'd secretly feared after her experience on Tojo that Dak didn't care who touched her.

"I need inside your channel," Dak said hoarsely as he carried her away. "I need in it more than I need air to breathe."

Geris could feel his solid erection against her hip. Her eyes widened when she realized that although he'd seen her naked more often than clothed, she had no idea what his penis looked like. But lordy, lordy it felt *big*.

She wrapped her arms around his neck, wondering what would come next. And, she thought dryly, whether or not she'd live through it.

Chapter 10

Geris had been informed prior to the Consummation Feast that Ari would be in the bedchamber with them tonight, but truth be told she didn't want the Chief Priestess's help. She wanted Dak all to herself with nobody there to bear witness.

"As soon as his rod is impaled within your channel, I shall take my leave," Ari whispered to her. "I am here but to aid you, my dear. Not to upset you."

Geris smiled at her. "Read my thoughts. You don't upset me. But I can't take…"

"I know." Ari grinned. "'Tis a jealous *heeka-beast* you are." She winked. "'Twill be all right. Some wenches enjoy watching what others do not. I will touch no body but yours. 'Tis a vow."

Geris blew out a breath. That much she could handle. It wasn't like she hadn't been groped by a lot of others up until this point, she thought grimly. Besides, there were worse things in life than having a drop-dead gorgeous woman massage various parts of your body. Like—sweet Jesus!—five *pugmuff* tongues licking you all over.

Ari's soft laughter echoed throughout the bedchamber as she helped Geris out of her white *qi'ka.* "You enjoyed it and well you know it. I can read your thoughts, aye?" She grinned. "They are a wicked talented race of males. Leastways, their tongues are."

Geris snorted at that. "I refuse to remember that evening fondly, thank you just the same."

"But you will always recall this moon-rising with a smile," she murmured. "'Twill be the best eve of your life."

Geris considered that as she climbed up onto the raised bed. Naked, she didn't bother to try and shield herself from the priestess. What was the point? Ari had already seen her naked in the bathing chamber.

"Lie down," Ari murmured as she summoned off her own clothing. Her puffy pink nipples stood out in contrast to her honey-tanned skin. "Your Sacred Mate is about to re-enter the bedchamber."

He did, not even thirty seconds later. Geris's eyes slightly widened when she saw him. She could never recall being more attracted to a man in her life. He looked larger than life, standing there at the foot of the bed with a possessive expression on his face. His breathing was ragged, perspiration already dotting his chest and forehead. Every muscle in his impressive body tensed as he drank in the sight of her, naked and waiting to be mounted by him.

"Lie all the way down," Ari murmured. "Spread your legs apart and offer your body to your mate."

She did as the Chief Priestess instructed, figuring the thousand-year-old woman would know what was best for Dak's peace of mind better than she did...a peace of mind Geris was quickly fearing was deserting him. The control he was wielding over his emotions was so tenuous it was beginning to frighten her. Her bridal necklace was pulsing so rapidly it made her nerves go on edge. His eyes were narrowed in a manner she'd never before seen, his hulking musculature corded and tensed.

Geris glanced away, unable to maintain eye contact. She had never behaved so docilely in her life, but she found herself immediately obeying Ari and lying on her back. She spread her legs wide open and exhaled.

"Not good enough," Ari whispered. "Not to a Trystonni male. Leastways, not to one so far gone."

Geris turned her head and gazed uncomprehendingly at her.

"Show your submission to him." When Geris narrowed her eyes, Ari placed two fingertips over her lips. "Shh. Do as you are bade or the mounting will be fierce wicked. Later you can handle that. This moon-rising you needs be mounted gently."

Her almond-shaped eyes widened. "What do I do?" This was beginning to get a little scary.

"Use your fingers to spread your pussy lips apart. Do not make eye contact."

"What if he still hurts me?" she fiercely whispered.

Ari ran a hand over her brow. "'Twill be all right."

The bridal necklace pulsed more rapidly. When a small growling sound emitted from Dak's throat, a sound very akin to a wild animal displaying dominance, Geris yelped and immediately spread apart her pussy lips.

Sweet Jesus!

Dak grunted in an arrogant, appeased manner that somehow made her feel better. It was like he was okay again, a state she wanted to keep him in until this was over. She released the breath she hadn't realized she'd been holding in. Good grief! She felt like she was about to be mounted by Cro-Magnon man!

The feel of the raised bed dipping slightly under the pressure of Dak's weight told Geris that he would be taking her at any moment. The sound of his leathers being discarded to the floor snagged her attention. Unable to resist a preview of what was about to enter her body, she braved a quick glance at his erect penis. She did a double take. She gasped.

Holy *shiiiiit!*

Dak dragged his gaze back from where the naked Chief Priestess sat next to him and leveled it onto his bride. He took in the sight of her tempting onyx body stretched out and splayed wide, ready to accommodate him, and his nostrils flared with the satisfaction of an accomplished hunter. His breathing was choppy, his control stretched.

'Twas time.

Dak summoned the clothes from his body, one golden eyebrow arching arrogantly when he heard his *nee'ka's* drawn-in breath at the sight of his fierce erection. "Aye?"

Geris licked her lips. Her almond-shaped eyes rounded disbelievingly. "Sweet Jesus," she muttered.

Dak grinned. "You know what they say, my hearts."

"W-What's that?"

"Once you go Dak, you never go back."

Geris believed him. Good lord in heaven how she believed him. She could only pray that she would manage to live through this night without being split in half. Unthinkingly, she released her pussy lips and clamped her hands to her forehead. "Uh, Ari...there is no way in the hell that thing will ever fit!"

The bridal necklace began to pulse red—anger. Her lips pinched together in a frown. "Dak!" she said, exasperated. "It's huge! I've seen baseball bats smaller than that!"

He grunted, the sound arrogant. "Leastways," he sniffed, "'tis for a certainty your Dot has no toys such as this one." He grabbed his penis by the base and squeezed. "Else pilgrims would trek to her doors at all hours, beseeching her to share of her prized treasure."

Geris rolled her eyes. Then she frowned. "How did you hear me talk about Dot from all the way across the..." She sighed. "Never mind. I'm sure I don't want to know. I guess it's true what they say about the size of a man's ears," she said grimly.

Ari chuckled. "Twill be all right, my queen."

"My ass it will!" She made to sit up. "Forget it!"

Dak's jaw clenched. His eyes narrowed a fraction of a second before Geris lost all control over her body. She gasped when she was thrust back down on the raised bed by forces unseen. As if she had been pinioned and tied by invisible ropes, her arms were thrown back over her head and her thighs were spread wide apart. Her nostrils flared. "You suck," she ground out.

Dak stared at her exposed cunt intensely, making her eyes widen, causing her anger to dissolve into worry. "I shall begin as I mean to go on," he declared in a firm tone as he drew closer. "No more shall I permit my love of the hearts for you to interfere with my law."

Geris's eyes narrowed. She refused to be swayed by his inadvertent declaration of love. Even if it was doing odd things to her heart. "Your law?"

"Aye. My law." He palmed her breasts and began to gently knead them.

"What is your law?" She frowned, disliking how good his hands felt there when she wanted to talk.

One dominant eyebrow rose, showing her a side of Dak she'd never before seen until this night. A side that made her feel a bit hesitant, a bit frightened of a man who until this moment she'd never feared in the slightest.

"You will do as you are bade by me, *nee'ka*," he said softly—too softly. "Always. Do I tell you to go to your rooms, you go without question. Do I tell you to bend o'er and accept a child's spanking as a punishment, you will do it. Do I tell you to spread your legs for my pleasure, you spread them." His jaw tightened. "This is my law."

Her teeth gritted. "Oh really."

"Aye," he growled. "Really."

"'Tis not the time for this," Ari murmured into her ear. "He is feeling nigh unto the animal for need of you. You can hold your own and well you know it. Fight later, join now."

Geris sighed. This was just too much. And yet she knew Ari was speaking the truth. Dak had a tangible desperateness to be inside of her, to brand her as it were. Perhaps after that branding took place he'd go back to acting like the man he'd been since the moment they'd first met. The man he'd been clear up until now.

The man she had fallen hopelessly in love with.

Because if he didn't she'd kill him in his sleep.

Dak nuzzled the inside of one of her thighs with his face. "I need you, *ty'ka*," he said hoarsely before kissing it. Rising up on his knees and grabbing her thighs with either hand, he placed the head of his erection at the opening of her vagina and began to slowly push inside. "And I love you," he murmured.

"Oh Dak," Geris breathed out. To actually hear those words on his lips made her feel a happiness inside she'd never expected to feel for a man. She shuddered, opening her mouth to give him the words back. She felt them too. And it was time to tell him. "I l—*aaaaaaaagggghhh!*"

Geris gasped, a numbing pain splintering through her insides, as Dak plunged his huge cock into her all the way to the hilt.

"So sorry," he muttered, his teeth gritting. His golden hair was soaked at the temples from perspiration. His eyes closed briefly. His breathing was ragged. "I tried to wait, but I—"

"Your Highness!" Ari chastised before thumping him soundly on the shoulder. "What do you to your *nee'ka*!"

He grunted. "'Tis wicked mean, this! I cannot go slow!" he bellowed.

The Chief Priestess tsk-tsked him but said nothing else. The damage had already been done. All they could hope for now was that Geris would recover from the shock of it soon.

Geris heard none of their fighting. She was too busy lying on her back, her eyes crossed—and not in a good way this time!—gaping dumbly as she came to terms with the fact that she'd just had a cock which felt the size of a small country impaled inside of her like nobody's business. "Oh. My. God."

Dak cradled her face, worry evident in his eyes and voice. He ran a hand through her micro-braids. "*Pani*, you are well? I have not split you asunder with my wicked beastie of a cock?"

From any other man that would have been a laughable question. From Dak, it was an appropriate one. "I. Am. Going. To. Kill. You," she bit out in a weak monotone, eyes still crossed.

He frowned.

Ari snorted. "Excellent work, Your Majesty. I would that I could witness more royal joinings go so smoothly as this one."

He grunted.

"Mayhap when you are done filling her womb with life-force we can take turns hitting her about the head with bottles of *matpow*."

His jaw clenched. "'Tis done, your part. I am all the way in. None can make a claim that I did not take her. Now be gone."

"Fine." Ari stood up, her lips pinched into a frown. "Summon me later if you mayhap wish to pin her to the wall that we might take turns blindfolding each other and throwing knives at her wee body as she spins about in a circular fashion. Mayhap after that we can—"

"I said be gone," Dak gritted out. "Shoo! Shoo!"

Ari raised an eyebrow. "Had I not aided your *mani* in the birthing of you, 'twould be a *zizi-bub* I zapped you into just now." She waved a dismissive hand even as her form began to shimmer and dissolve. "May the goddess be with you, my queen." When nothing of the Chief Priestess was left visible except for her face, she halted the process of dissolving long enough to smile gamine-like at Dak. "And may the goddess be with you, my king, when the queen is released from her trance and she is able to move about." Her eyebrows rose. "And get her hands on you."

Dak frowned at her dissolving image. The sound of fading, trill laughter perfumed the air. "Geris would not dare strike me," he muttered. "'Tis blasphemous to suggest as much—ouch!" Dak gritted his teeth as he grabbed at the eye that might end up going black and blue. "How did you exit from your trance?" he growled. "And why did you hit me thusly? My bedamned eye is sore!"

"Now you know how I feel!" Geris seethed. "And Ari released me from it!"

"Ger-*is*!"

"Oh shut-up!"

Joined together in the most intimate possible way, Dak's cock buried deep inside Geris's body, they bickered back and forth for another five minutes. By the time they'd finished, the absurdity of the situation at last got to both of them. They began laughing.

He smiled. "'Tis sorry I am, *nee'ka*. Leastways, I needed to be inside of you."

She smiled back. "And I'm sorry I hit you." She frowned. "But don't ever pull any junk like that again."

"'Tis a vow I will not."

"Good," she murmured. Her eyelids grew heavy. "By the way, I think I've adjusted to the size of you, you know."

He raised an eyebrow. "Hmm." Coming down on top of her, he put his elbows at either side of her head. "And what would you like me to do about that?" he asked thickly.

She palmed his steely buttocks and squeezed. "I think you already know," she whispered.

Dak's eyes glazed over as he raised his hips, slightly withdrew his cock, and slowly pushed it back inside of her wet pussy. She hissed, the encouraging sound making his teeth grit and his balls tighten.

He began to slowly rock in and out of her. "Your channel feels so good," he said, his voice hoarse. In and out. Back and forth. Nice and slow... "So bewitching."

Geris moaned, her head falling back against the pillows as he palmed her breasts. She shivered when his thumbs and index fingers found her dark, sensitive nipples and began massaging them from root to tip. "Oh god."

His cock filled her all up, made her damn near come with every stroke, yet left her wanting more of it...and of him. "Harder," she gasped as she reared up and clamped her legs around his hips. *More.*

"I'll give you more," he ground out as he picked up the pace. His nostrils flared at the sound of her low moans. "I love fucking my pussy."

"Dak..."

"My pussy," he said over and over again as he rode her faster, pumping in and out of her cunt in possessive strokes. His jaw was clenched, the veins in his massive arms bulging, as he plunged in and out of her. He rotated his hips, grinding their crotches together, making her moan with pleasure as he filled her all up. "All mine," he said thickly.

"*Shit.*"

He fucked her harder, the sound of flesh slapping against flesh echoing throughout the bedchamber. His muscles tensed as he rode her, violently pumping away inside of her. He continued to knead her breasts, plumping up the already stiff nipples. His eyes closed as he moaned low in his throat, the expression on his face reminiscent of a virginal boy who'd gotten to fuck his first pussy.

"*Oh my god – Dak. I'm coming!*" Geris groaned as she prepared to climax, pleasure knotting in her belly. She instinctively raised her hips, wanting as much friction against her cunt as possible. "*Oh god.*"

She came long and loud, her nipples stabbing up to hit his palms. His teeth gritted, the exquisite feel of her pussy trying to milk his cock almost his undoing. He had wanted the first time to last all night. He would be lucky to make it last ten minutes.

"As am I, *nee'ka*," he panted, plunging in and out of her cunt in hard, branding strokes. His nostrils flared as he grew closer toward the inevitable climax he was trying to stave off, but he couldn't open his eyes to save his life. He squeezed them shut tighter instead, animalistically mating her on the raised bed. Her pussy felt tight, warm, and inviting. And all his.

He fucked her impossibly harder, growling low in his throat, his eyes at last opening. He rotated his hips and slammed her harder, sinking into her cunt in lightning quick motions.

Geris screamed, instantaneously coming from the hard, deep pounding. Dak's teeth gritted as her pussy walls contracted again, and this time he knew he was a goner.

He pumped her harder. Once. Twice. Three times more...

"Geris!" He bellowed out her name as he climaxed, hot seed spurting deep into her womb. He growled as his balls tried to empty, flesh slapping flesh, his cock still violently rooting away inside of her cunt, not willing to stop fucking her.

The bridal necklace began to pulse, inducing Geris's eyes to widen. "What the—*oooooohhhhhh!*"

Geris moaned and groaned, her head falling back into the pillows again, as a series of the most intense, numbing orgasms ripped through her belly like a tidal wave.

"Oh my god!" she screamed. *"Oh my god!"*

Dak growled into her ear as he frenziedly fucked her, her climaxes making his teeth grit. He groaned out her name as he came again, his entire body shuddering and convulsing atop hers.

Their breathing harsh, sweat soaking their bodies, they held onto each other as they slowly came down from the mutual climactic high. Later—much later—when their breathing had somewhat slowed, Dak moved off of her body and to the *vesha* hides beside her. He drew her into his side, holding her closely and tenderly.

He chuckled as he took in her expression. "Mayhap you will no longer think to bedevil me, wily wench." When she didn't say anything, simply laid there with her eyes once again crossed, his smile spread. "Let us ask your Dot has she ever beheld such a superior man-part as this one."

"Nyooo nyooomph."

Dak chuckled at the nonsensical sound. Then he cuddled his wife closer and fell asleep, leaving Geris to stare at the ceiling, her mouth agape and her mind gone to mush.

She smiled slowly, her eyes still crossed like a lunatic's.

Once you go Dak you never go back. Uh-uh. No way.

Sweeeeeet Jesus!

Chapter 11

Meanwhile, on the green moon Ti Q'won...

Jek strolled into the bedchamber, his pace brisk. The giant, Yar'at, was lying on the raised bed, still unconscious. Three naked priestesses were attending to him, softly chanting whilst they rubbed liquidated healing sand all over his back, buttocks, and thighs.

The high lord came to a standstill at the foot of the bed. He didn't interrupt the goings-on, merely watched. Two bound servants quietly escorted him to a nearby *vesha* bench to offer him a distraction whilst he waited. He pulled down his leathers and took a seat. The buxom blondes immediately fell to their knees, one of them suckling his rigid shaft and the other one suckling his man sac. Jek leaned back on the bench with a sigh, his fingers idly sifting through either blonde's head whilst they sucked on him.

Fifteen minutes later, Yar'at was turned over and the process was repeated to his front. The priestesses continued their lulling chant, liquid healing sand rubbed into his chest, over his legs, and up and down the length of his erect cock and tight man sac. They repeatedly masturbated him as he laid there, the giant softly groaning as he flickered in and out of consciousness.

It was another hour before the priestesses finished. When finally they did, Yar'at had been depleted of life-force twelve times, Jek but three. The giant's coloring was less pale, more normal. His breathing, though asleep, was relaxed and even.

The leader amongst the priestesses walked to where Jek sat, stood before him, and inclined her head. She was tall, brunette, and busty. Her nipples were a startling, pleasing rouge contrasted against honey-colored skin. "Milord."

"Milady."

The bound servants scurried away, not wanting to interrupt. Jek was about to put his cock away when the priestess made a motion with her hand not to. He raised an eyebrow. She smiled softly, then slowly straddled the bench and his lap.

"I thought we could both use this," she breathed out.

Jek's gaze grew heavy-lidded as she lowered the opening of her wet pussy onto the head of his thick cock. "How is he?"

"Much better." The priestess closed her eyes, impaling herself on his jutting erection with a gasp. He gritted his teeth. She opened her eyes. "Sleeping, but well. 'Twill be mayhap another fortnight or more before he's completely healed."

"But he will heal?" He palmed her buttocks, kneading them as she slowly rode up and down the length of his manhood. "I must return to Sand City with all speed. I should like some assurances before I take my leave yet again."

"Aye. For a certainty he shall heal."

Jek nodded, appeased. He sucked in his breath as the priestess' riding picked up in pace. "You will heal Yar'at with your tight channel, aye?"

"Aye," she breathed out, riding faster. Her head fell back, lulling against her neck. "We shall give him as much pussy as he can handle and then some."

Jek pulled her in closer and smashed his face into her large breasts. He closed his eyes, sucking on her nipples whilst she rode him.

They fucked for over an hour, both in her cunt and in her arse. By the time they pulled away from each other, spent and replete, Jek had to leave for Sand City. He checked one last time on Yar'at, murmured to the giant that he would return the soonest, and took his leave.

Chapter 12

For seven days and seven nights he fucked her. Over and over. Again and again. He made her scream, moan, beg, convulse...

Geris took him in every hole, accepted him in every imaginable (and unimaginable) position. She sucked him off so many times she lost count. And yet his desire to be inside of her never lessened. It only seemed to intensify.

"Dak," she groaned. "I can't take any more." On her back, Geris glanced down to where their bodies were joined, to where his lightly tanned cock was repeatedly sinking into her pussy over and over again. The contrast in skin tones was arousing. And beautiful. Almost like a choreographed ballet where the director tries to heighten the impact of the piece by contrasting different gyrations and colors before the viewing audience.

"It feels so good," he murmured, his eyes heavy-lidded. He gritted his teeth as he watched his cock plunge into her cunt. "I never wish to cease this."

She half moaned and half laughed. "If we don't, I'll die. I need something to drink." Her lips pinched into a frown. "And no more of that *matpow* junk either. I prefer the juice."

Dak sighed like a martyr, but relented a few strokes later. "Your pleasure is mine, *nee'ka*." He bent his neck and kissed her sweetly on the tip of the nose.

Raising his head, he stared down at her for a long moment. Geris searched his eyes, knowing he was wanting to tell her that he loved her. She hoped he would because she still hadn't said the words back to him and wanted the perfect excuse to tell him how she felt. She didn't know why she couldn't bring herself to say them without prompting—she supposed she was still feeling a bit vulnerable and cowardly where these new emotions she was experiencing were concerned.

Dak cleared his throat and glanced away. Geris took a deep breath, hoping she didn't look as disappointed as she felt. *Just say it to him, Geris. Say the words!*

"I suppose 'tis best do we call for food and drink, my hearts."

He rolled off of her and sat on the edge of the bed, his back to her. Her gaze drank in the sight of his powerful back and the beginnings of his muscled buttocks. Unable to resist, she reached over and lightly tongued the two dimples denting the top of either cheek.

Dak chuckled. "'Tis not the actions a wench undesirous of a good rut."

She grinned as she raised her head. "Can't help it. You have got what we call on earth a 'killer bod'."

He turned his head and smiled, that gorgeous dimple popping out. "Aye?"

Her smile faded as she stared at the beauty of his face. She swallowed around the lump of emotion in her throat. "Aye," she whispered.

Dak raised an eyebrow. "*Nee'ka*? Is aught amiss? You look—"

"I love you." She took a deep breath and blew it out when she saw his eyes widen. "Very much," she murmured.

"Ah *nee'ka*...!" Dak was so excited about the revelation that he forgot himself. Without thinking, he used his powers to snatch her bodily up from the bed and whisk her into his arms.

"*Eeeek!*" Geris screeched as she took off, made a quick veer to the left, then tumbled into his embrace. She slapped him soundly on the chest. "Dak!" But his smile was so wide she couldn't help but to chuckle.

"I love you too," he said happily, hugging her so tightly she could scarcely breathe.

"Good," she rasped out, her eyes bulging.

"Oh. Sorry, my hearts." Dak released his hold on her a bit, enough to permit her to breathe normally again. "It feels like forever that I waited to hear you say those words."

Geris grinned from over his shoulder. "Just don't expect me to go shouting it from the mountaintops yet. I'm new at this in-love business."

Dak chuckled. "As am I."

They hugged for a few quiet minutes, both of them enjoying the newfound intimacy that could rival the pulsing of any bridal necklace. Eventually, however, Dak begrudgingly released her, set her on the crystal floor, and stood up. "I will call for food and drink anon," he sighed. "Leastways, you should probably go visit with Kyra for a time because we must venture on to our holding in two moon-risings."

Geris's eyes widened. "The green moon?"

"Aye. Ti Q'won."

She absently nodded. "Will I see Kyra again soon?" she whispered.

Dak stilled. He turned to face her. "Aye. Of course. You think me an ogre?"

She teasingly harrumphed. "Well, only sometimes."

He winked. "Get you into a pretty *qi'ka* and enjoy your time with Kyra." He strode away, his naked, ultra-masculine body again drawing her attention. "I will fetch you from the great hall later."

* * * * *

It had been, to say the least, an eventful two days for Geris. Not even an hour after she'd left Dak in their rooms and went to visit with Kyra—her first excursion out of the apartments since she and Dak had joined—her best friend had given birth to twins. The scary part was nobody had even realized Kyra was pregnant. Who would have ever thought that the gestation period on Tryston was only three weeks!

Sweet Jesus, it had been ugly. Like something out of a nightmare, glowing blue junk had rushed out from between Kyra's thighs and gone everywhere. Within minutes she had started hatching an egg—an egg!

119

After the shock and horror of it all had passed, however, Geris's heart had damn near wrenched into halves at the joy she'd experienced holding her best friend's twin daughters in her arms. She and Kyra were so close, like sisters, that the poignant moment had been like holding one of her own. She hadn't ever wanted to let go. They'd felt so warm and delicate and snuggly.

In retrospect, she was grateful that fate had seen fit to make sure she was present before Kyra gave birth. She couldn't imagine having missed Zora and Zara's hatchings for the world.

She was also grateful for having those two days to spend almost exclusively with her best friend for they'd had a lot to catch up on. It was amazing to think that what had been only three weeks to Kyra had been three years to Geris. Even if Dak hadn't sped up their arrival via that portal in deep space they'd passed through, it still would have only been a few months. Amazing.

But now it was time to go home. *Home.* Geris shook her head and smiled. Two weeks ago home had been earth. An earth she felt no particular attachment to without Kyra there. But now home was a green, low-hanging moon she'd never before laid eyes on. She was as excited as she was nervous.

What if she didn't like it there? How could she ever tell Dak that the home he took so much pride in wasn't a place she wanted to live? These thoughts plagued her as she made her way toward where she knew her husband would be waiting on her.

Walking toward the great hall, her thoughts were a million miles away. The sound of male laughter, however, managed to snag her attention.

"Do not be a dunce," Zor said dryly to Dak, rolling his eyes. "The rebel leader could not possibly be hiding out on Morak."

"Mine own colony?" Kil said arrogantly. "Do not be a lackwit!"

Dak smiled, though his eyes were sad. Geris winced, able to feel his emotions as though they were her own.

Her husband, she thought sadly, was hurting. He actually thought his brothers were serious when they called him names. What was good-natured jesting to Zor and Kil, Dak took to heart, believing it. But how could his own brothers not realize they were hurting him? she thought angrily. It didn't take a bridal necklace to see how crestfallen he looked.

Geris permitted the ribbing to go on another minute more before she strolled into the great hall, her head held high. "I'm ready to go, Dak," she said, her nostrils flaring. She narrowed her eyes at her brothers-in-law. "I'm tired of being in this place."

Zor and Kil looked at each other quizzically. "Is aught amiss?" Zor asked, perplexed. "Did you and Kyra mayhap have a spat?"

Geris snorted at that. "I don't think so. You see, Zor, Kyra and I love each other. Therefore, we care about each other's feelings."

"*Nee'ka...*"

Her chin thrust up. "We don't spew things at each other without stopping to think about how hurtful untrue words can be."

Zor and Kil shared another confused look.

Dak sighed. "'Tis all right, wee one. Let us just go, aye?"

"What is all right?" Kil asked, his gaze flicking back and forth between his brother and sister-in-law.

"No, it's not all right," Geris said on a frown leveled at Dak's brothers. "But yeah, let's go."

"Now wait just a second!" Zor said firmly as the couple began to walk away. "Geris Q'ana Tal, I demand to know of what you speak."

She turned around on her heel and narrowed her eyes. Dak took a deep breath and blew it out, realizing as he must have that she wouldn't back down until she'd said her piece. Huffing, she threw a hand at Zor. "Why do you always refer to him as 'dunce', 'lackwit', and all of those other names any fool could see hurts his feelings?"

Zor's eyes narrowed. "You think me a fool?"

Kil rolled his eyes. "'Tis not the bedamned point!" He sighed and turned to his younger brother. "Dak," he murmured. "'Tis but the way we've jested with you since we were boys."

"You are the little brother," Zor said in way of explanation.

"Well stop," Geris said quietly. "It hurts. And furthermore, it's not true. If he says to look on Morak for…well, whoever it was you mentioned…then perhaps you should."

Dak's eyes glittered with emotion as he looked at her, though Geris couldn't see that. She was too busy glaring daggers at his brothers.

"Point taken," Zor murmured.

Kil clapped Dak on the back. "My apologies, brother. How could you not know we were but jesting? Any fool, as your *nee'ka* so aptly called us, can see that you are a warlord to be reckoned with."

Dak, unused to such praise-filled words from them, clearly didn't know what to say. "I—well, thank you," he grumbled.

"'Tis true," Zor said matter-of-factly. "Ti Q'won is the only of our holdings never once broached by insurrectionist sympathizers. 'Tis a reason for that."

Geris beamed with happiness for her husband as she listened to the exchange. It was readily apparent that Dak had needed this verbal validation. Like his brothers, she couldn't imagine why he would have ever thought they were serious about him being a dunce either, but she supposed everyone, even a giant, has their insecurities. Somehow that knowledge made her feel less twit-like for holding back on telling her husband that she loved him. He was vulnerable too. But in different ways.

By the time they left the Palace of the Dunes, Dak was chuckling. He winked down at her, his arm drawing her close against his side. "If ever those rebel sympathizers had thought to broach Ti Q'won, they will think again do they learn of the fierce *nee'ka* who rules at my side."

Geris smiled, vastly content. Sweet Jesus, how she loved this man.

Chapter 13

Yar'at awoke in a foreign place to the feel of three naked wenches kissing all over his body. He blinked a few times, forcing his eyes open, deciding that he must be dreaming. 'Twas the only explanation he could summon, for he'd never before lain with a woman. He'd dreamt of it more oft than he could count, yet never had he been given the opportunity.

His eyes opened. He stilled.

He was awake and yet the wenches were still here.

A golden-haired wench smiled up to him as she put the head of his stiff cock into her lovely mouth. Yar'at sucked in his breath, his breathing rapidly growing labored. "Who are y-you?" he stammered out. He swallowed roughly as he watched her lips go down further on his shaft. His stomach muscles clenched.

She didn't answer him, but then she didn't need to, for Yar'at's gaze fell down the bed toward a busty brunette who was crawling towards him. The naked beauty wore the ankle chain of a priestess—an emblem declaring her a slave to the goddess.

Before he could think to ask why 'twas he was being attended to, the golden-haired wench took his cock as far into her throat as was possible and sucked up and down the length of him. He gasped as she suckled him, his teeth clenching, the feeling more exquisite than ever he'd dreamt it would be.

The need to close his eyes and bask in the pleasure offered to him was overwhelming, but more powerful than that was the desire to watch a cock he'd thought not worthy of a wench's ministrations be attended to as though 'twas the most wondrous thing in the goddess' creation. The soft moans of pleasure erupting from the priestess' throat as she sucked on him was headier than anything he'd ever before known.

A second golden-haired priestess latched her mouth around his man-sac and sucked on it whilst the first one suckled his staff faster and faster. Yar'at groaned, his head falling back, no longer able to keep his eyes open.

A plump nipple was popped into his mouth. He suckled it hard, his breathing labored, as the two priestesses attending to his cock and balls made him feel things a man sold to a mine-master as a boy-child had never thought to feel. The brunette, whose nipple his lips were clamped around, cradled his head against her chest and whispered soothing words into his ear.

He didn't want to spurt for fear 'twould end.

"'Tis all right, handsome one," the brunette priestess murmured. "Give them your life-force. We will not leave you until you've been milked dry does it take weeks."

Yar'at groaned from around the delicious nipple. And then he spurted, his life-force spewing into a hungry, awaiting mouth.

Stars exploded behind his eyes as he moaned, but he never released the nipple. He suckled it harder and harder still, until the brunette sucked in her breath and begged him to fuck her.

By the sands, he thought, his cock stiffer than he'd thought possible, he had to be dreaming. How could this be real, a beautiful woman begging the likes of him to fuck her...

But fuck her he did. As soon as the golden-haired priestesses released his cock from their mouths, he quickly flipped over, pulled the brunette beneath him, and sank his jutting erection into her tight, warm cunt. He groaned long and loudly, at last knowing the feel of a welcoming pussy.

She gasped when he entered her, the sound like music to his ears. The brunette's eyelids were heavy with arousal as she wrapped her legs around his hips. "Long and hard," she murmured.

Yar'at swallowed roughly. "M-Milady?"

She squeezed him with her thighs. "Fuck me long and hard," she breathed out. "You've a gloriously huge man-part, handsome one."

His nostrils flaring, Yar'at plunged into her cunt, seating himself to the hilt. When she gasped again in her pleasure, he took it as a good sign and began to stroke in and out of her in the way he'd oft dreamt of doing to a wench.

He slammed into her pussy harder and harder, faster and faster. He moaned as he fucked her, his eyes closing from the bliss of it. It occurred to him how wondrous 'twould feel if he could suck on her nipple whilst plunging in and out of her cunt. And then, as if the priestesses could anticipate his every thought and sought to make his fantasies reality, a ripe rouge nipple was there for him to suckle of.

Yar'at suckled of it. It tasted like bliss. He suckled it hard until she too was moaning and he thought he'd died of pleasure and gone through the Rah. 'Twas heady indeed that two wenches were moaning because of him—the wench he was fucking and the one he was sucking.

Before he could help himself he was spurting again, his seed emptying into the brunette's tempting channel. He feared for a moment that the bliss would be over, but as soon as he climbed off of her and laid back down on the bed, one of the golden-haired wenches impaled herself upon his still erect rod.

His jaw clenched as he watched her pink pussy envelope his stiff cock over and over, again and again. He watched her for as long as he was able, until the other golden-haired priestess lowered her cunt down onto his face and began riding him.

Yar'at groaned as he clamped his lips around her clit and sucked at her pussy to his hearts' content. She came for him at least three times, and he hungrily drank her up, whilst the other priestess rode his swollen cock, bouncing up and down on him as her tits jiggled and she breathily moaned.

'Twould be two more moon-risings of healing sand massages and spurting in the priestesses' various holes before he began to feel his health semi-restored. He feared they would be leaving him as soon as he was better, but knew too that he could not be selfish for like as naught they had others to heal as well.

"Fear not," handsome one, the brunette said to him on the second night when he was buried deep inside of her arsehole pumping away like a crazed gulch beast. "We shall stay with you for a fortnight, fulfilling your every need and quenching your every desire."

"Hurry up and finish fucking her," a golden-haired priestess mused to Yar'at concerning the brunette. "I should like some more of that stiff cock as well."

Yar'at whimpered. 'Twas for a certainty he had died and gone to the heavens.

Chapter 14

Ti Q'won took a little getting used to. Okay, a lot of getting used to. But Geris ended up loving her new home. It took some settling in to grow accustomed to being called "Your Highness", to having half naked women scurry around to do your bidding, and to have *Kefa* slaves eat you out every time you unthinkingly got naked in their presence! — but all in all the low-hanging green moon was a wonderful place to live.

Dak being Dak, he still couldn't keep his hands off of her. Nor did he try. Nor did she want him to try.

On the second day following their arrival, Geris went out strolling about the castle grounds while Dak attended to some political business he was hell-bent on seeing to. He was always secretive about stuff like that, but since she'd never been all that interested in politics anyway, she let it ride.

She smiled to herself as she scoped out the castle grounds, taking in the beauty of her surroundings. The grass-like stuff that covered the terrain was silky soft and the most vivid jade-green Geris had ever beheld. Turning to face her home, she smiled at the huge green crystal structure that jutted upwards from a swirling mist, rivaling Emerald City in its glory.

"So beautiful," she whispered as she simply stared at it. "So incred —"

The sound of a low growl made her eyes widen. What the…?

Her breathing stilled when the low growl was joined by another. And then another. And — oh damn — *another.*

Geris gulped, afraid to turn around. There was something eerily familiar about that growling sound…

Her eyes widened in comprehension at the precise moment she was attacked. She screamed as she was tackled to the ground, the black *qi'ka* she wore shredded from her body within seconds. Naked and defenseless, her thighs were thrust wide apart, giving the predators access to what it was they wanted.

Geris's eyes crossed as four Rustian faces dove for her pussy. She had asked Dak if these creatures were indigenous to Sand City. He had said no. Unfortunately, when she'd failed to ask specifically about the moon of Ti Q'won, he hadn't been forthcoming with this very important, *needed-to-know* information!

"I. Am. Going. To. Kill. Him," she bit out in a weak monotone. "Why. Does. Every. Thing. Want. To. Eat. Me. Out," she seethed.

The little guys on Ti Q'won were even more voracious eaters than the ones on Tojo had been, she soon discovered. They snorted into her cunt like pigs, greedily sucking on her clit until she gasped and groaned, orgasming again and again and again. By the time they bodily pulled her under a nearby bush, most likely so she wouldn't be found until they'd had their fill of cunt-juice, she was so weak from climaxing that she couldn't offer them the least bit of resistance.

They looked tougher than the Rustians of Tojo as well, she thought grimly. They were only a foot tall, but more muscular and powerful looking. Good grief, some of them even had tattoos! It was like she'd been kidnapped by a band of handsome, but too-stupid-to-live, foot-high sailors.

Once she'd been securely hidden under the bush, they feasted on her pussy like mad. These Rustians liked sucking on nipples too she quickly learned, for throughout the entire hours-long ordeal there was always a Rustian mouth clamped around either one sucking away like crazy.

She gasped and groaned. Her head fell back and her nipples stiffened as they frenziedly sucked on her cunt. When those four were finished there were four more. And then another pack of four. And then another and another.

The sound of gluttonous munching, slurping, and—oh sweet Jesus they were belching when they finished!—reached her ears over and over, again and again. By the time a worried Dak found her four hours later and scared off the remaining little guys from the fifth pack that had dined on her, Geris feared her eyes would never uncross again.

"Ah *nee'ka*," Dak crooned. "I mayhap should have warned you never to leave the castle without a warrior to keep them away from you. Leastways, the cunt-juice predators here are fierce wicked, yet contained they are to outside of the castle."

"Nyoooo nyyyyyyoooooooomph!"

Dak grimaced. He was fairly certain another black eye was in his near future.

* * * * *

"Ouch!" Dak gritted his teeth as he grabbed at the eye that might end up going black and blue. "Why did you hit me thusly?" he growled. "My bedamned eye is sore!"

"Now you know how my pussy feels!" Geris seethed. "I asked you if you had Rustians here and you said no!"

"You asked me about Sand City! You did not ask me about Ti Q'won!"

"You suck!"

"Ger-*is*!"

"Oh shut-up!"

* * * * *

It had taken Geris two days to recover, but much to Dak's surprise, only an hour of swear words and striking him afore she had forgiven him. She had ended up laughing over the whole incident, recalling how the wee things had gone so far as to hide her under a bush so she wouldn't be found.

Dak sighed, shaking his head. Her moods were forever a surprise. He smiled, deciding that was mayhap not such a bad thing. For a certainty it was superior to giving him black eyes, he mentally grumbled.

On the fourth evening following their arrival, the king and queen sat out on the balcony adjoined to their personal apartments. Planet Tryston could be seen in the distance, a gold, shimmering mass slowly sinking below the horizon. The dominant red moon Morak was further away, an almost invisible red mark tinting the darkening sky.

Geris was on Dak's lap, her back to his front, her legs spread wide and his cock impaled in her pussy. One of his hands toyed with her nipples, massaging and elongating them, the other hand with her clit, arousing her beyond belief, as he placed shiver-inducing kisses all over her neck and shoulders. Wisely, he chose not to remind her of the Rustians.

Geris sucked in her breath. "That feels so good," she whispered. "God, Dak. You're so sexy and—"

"Pardon the interruption, Mighty One. I was told I would mayhap find you here."

Dak grunted. He had waited two nigh unto torturous moon-risings to get inside of her and now—

Geris yelped, startled. When she saw it was Jek, the warrior who had orally pleasured her at the Consummation Feast, she glanced away, embarrassed. "Let me up, Dak," she said. "I'm naked and we're having sex!"

He grunted as if to say "do you think I am not aware of this?" but didn't let her up. He held her tightly, his hand still stroking her pussy while he raised an eyebrow to Jek. "Aye?"

Jek's eyes strayed to Geris's exposed cunt. His eyelids grew heavy and the beginnings of an erection noticeably formed in his leathers before he looked away. Geris whimpered, deciding there were some things—like this!—about Trystonni life that she'd never get used to. Sweet Jesus!

But after that brief, lusty glance Jek gave her, he thankfully turned his attention to Dak. "You have been told of the giant Yar'at's arrival here, Mighty One?"

"Aye." Dak's eyes narrowed. "The last I saw of him he looked to be healing well enough by aid of the priestesses. Is aught amiss?"

Jek shook his head. "Nay. He is healing."

"Then...?"

"You have heard it be said he is a lackwit?"

Dak stilled, wondering where this conversation was going. He released Geris then, letting her have her way and close her legs. He sat her on his heavily muscled thigh instead and turned back to the high lord whilst she clung to him. He played with one of her breasts, massaging the nipple, as they conversed. "I have heard it be said. What's the meaning of your questions, cousin?"

Jek hesitated. "Have you spoken with him afore, Your Highness?"

"Aye." Dak frowned. "He is slow of the tongue but I do not think his thought processes challenged."

"Definitely not." Geris shook her head. "We spoke at lunch a great deal while Dak was out seeing to something or another. It took him a while to feel comfortable enough to speak to me, but once he realized I wasn't going to poke fun of his speech impediment he spoke to me freely. He's smart as a whip."

Jek seemed pleased by her evaluation.

Dak sighed. "I care not for riddles. What is the meaning of this inquisition, cousin?" He frowned as he glanced to Geris. "And why in the sands were you breaking your fast unattended with a male not of my line?"

Geris frowned back. "Because I felt like it. Besides, he's a guest here and he hasn't been in the best of health."

Dak gave her a look that said they'd speak more on the subject later. Geris gave him one back that said no, they wouldn't. He grunted and turned back to Jek.

"'Tis not a riddle I put to you, Mighty One, but a request."

"Which is what?" Dak asked.

Jek hesitated, then blew out a breath and came to the point. "I think Yar'at would make a fine warrior. Mayhap even more one day." When the king didn't make jest of his pronouncement he added, "And I request that you train him in my stead, my king, until

I have finished my duties under His Excellence the High King and am legally able to take Yar'at under mine own instruction."

Dak frowned. "Finding that he does not lack his wits and declaring him a warrior in the making are not necessarily one and the same. You best give unto me a better argument than this, cousin. My squadrons are already nigh unto overflowing."

"Dak!" Geris chastised.

He sighed. "*Nee'ka*, must you always interfere?"

"Yes!"

He muttered something under his breath, then regarded Jek. He knew his cousin understood his meaning even if his wife thought him cold-hearted. Warriors were the finest breed of Trystonni. The protectors of their people and the defenders of their way of life. Credits would be spent training none but the elite. That didn't mean Dak intended to throw Yar'at out on the streets, however.

Jek inclined his head. "You have been given a report on the state of the crystal silius mines. And," he quickly added when he could see anger growing on Dak's face, "you are already awares that I sent in the high lords of the sectors in question to set things to rights as soon as I knew of it."

Dak's nostrils flared. "'Tis disgraceful that the high lords knew naught of it. 'Tis why there are there to begin with for I cannot be in all places at all times. If they cannot be my eyes and ears, then who can," he muttered.

Jek snorted. "They fear your wrath for a certainty."

"As well they should. This issue has not been forgotten. Delayed until they set the situation to rights, but not forgotten."

"By all reports the mines are atrocious places. The majority of the workers die, retarded of mind or no, after less than three Yessat years in illegal slavery."

"That's awful," Geris whispered. She cuddled in closer to her husband. "It breaks my heart to even think about it."

Jek nodded. His gaze clashed with Dak's. "Yar'at lasted *ten* years."

Dak's eyebrows shot up. "Ten?"

"Aye, sire. Ten."

The king was quiet for a moment. "I begin to see your point," he finally conceded.

"You will train him in my stead then?"

Dak considered the question only a moment before inclining his head. "Aye. Your request is accepted."

Jek smiled. "'Twill not be forgotten, your kindness." He bowed, then turned on his heel to leave.

"Cousin," Dak called out.

Jek turned. "Aye?"

Dak's forehead wrinkled. "Why do you care so mightily? 'Tis a good thing, of course. But why?"

Jek was quiet for a long moment as he considered the question that had been put to him. Eventually he shrugged. "I truly do not know. A gut feeling perhaps. An intuition of sorts."

"About?"

Jek's gaze found his cousin's. "'Tis his destiny, this. I know not why, only that he must be trained."

Chapter 15

Two weeks later, naked and straddling Dak's lap in the raised bed, Geris gasped and grabbed her belly.

"*Nee'ka*?" Dak asked, worried. His eyes widened as he clutched her hips. "What ails you, my hearts?"

When she didn't respond right away, he made to sit up, but she pushed him back down on the bed. A smile slowly spread across her face. "Guess what?" she whispered.

"What?" he asked, searching her gaze.

Geris grinned. "Guess who's got the belly flutters?" she murmured.

That adorable dimple popped out on Dak's cheek. He pulled her face down and kissed her sweetly, his hands threading through her micro-braids. "I am to be a papa?" he whispered, his voice shaky.

A tear formed in her eye. "Yeah. The best one in any galaxy anywhere I bet."

"Oh," he rumbled, embarrassed. "I cannot say the best. I—" His eyebrows rose. "Well…mayhap." He grunted, an arrogant sound. "Leastways, 'tis probably correct you are."

Geris chuckled as she spread her naked body out on top of his. "Pilgrams will trek the world over to see the prized treasure I have in you."

Dak's eyes danced with humor, recalling as he did that those were almost the same words he'd used in regards to his wicked-big cock the eve that he'd joined his body to his wife's. He kissed her on the lips, then lifted his gaze to hers, his expression growing serious. "'Tis you that are the prized treasure, *nee'ka*. 'Tis you."

* * * * *

Having returned to Sand City as soon as the belly flutters began for reasons Dak never truly explained, Kyra held one of Geris's hands and Kil the other as the entire royal family waited for the hatching of the incubating *pani* sac Dak was cradling. Zor sat on the bed beside Kyra, Rem on the other side of Kil. All six of them maintained a hushed, reverent silence as they waited to find out the verdict.

"I wonder what it'll be," Kyra whispered.

"I don't know," Geris breathed out, "but the suspense is killing me."

"Look," Kil murmured. A grin tugged at the corners of his mouth. "'Tis starting to wiggle."

Sure enough, Geris could see two tiny hands and two tiny feet kicking and flailing at the sac surrounding them. She held her breath, her eyes wide, as she and Dak exchanged an excited look.

Two minutes later, tears streamed down Geris's face as the *pani* sac hatched and the most beautiful baby girl she'd ever laid eyes on kicked and screamed her way into the world. Her gorgeous face with features so much like Dak's were scrunched up into an angry little ball as she wailed against the fates that had snatched her from the dark, warm *pani* sac and into the brightly lit world of Tryston.

Her eyes were a startling, wizened blue, the same as her father's. Eyes that seemed as though they had the ability to look directly into your soul and claim a piece of it as their own. A tuft of golden hair sat on top of her head, giving the wizened look a touch of the devilish little gnome.

"She's perfect," Dak whispered, his eyes tearing up.

"Oh God, Ger, she's gorgeous," Kyra murmured, her own eyes doing a little tearing.

"A beauty," Rem pronounced, his gaze looking so hopeful. "Mayhap the goddess will see fit to bless me with one just like her someday."

Geris sucked in a breath as Dak handed her their firstborn daughter. "Oh wow," she quietly laughed, still partially crying. "Oh Dak, she's so perfect."

"Aye," he murmured. He kissed the tip of her nose. "Like you."

Geris kissed him back, then turned her undivided attention back to their new daughter. She had never before experienced feelings so overwhelming as this. The emotions she felt toward Dak were just as strong, but different. There was something indescribably humbling about holding the child you'd given birth to in your arms. Something that gave life and fate both sense and meaning.

The man she loved more than life itself sitting before her, the best friend she loved just as much but in a different way at her side, and her new, cherished baby girl laying in her arms...what more could a woman ask for?

Geris and Kyra exchanged a tearful, knowing look, both of them realizing how wonderful life had turned out to be. They had been reunited, they had been found — okay kidnapped! — by the loves of their lives, and they'd been blessed with precious children who would grow up to be as close as she and Kyra were. Somehow they both knew that would be the case.

"Come," Zor said quietly to the room at large. He winked at Geris. "Let us give the new *mani* and papa time alone afore they are obliged to name the wee beauty."

Kyra smiled as she stood up. "I'll be back," she murmured. "Call us when you're ready for visitors."

After everyone had left, Geris and Dak sat alone on the raised bed, holding and cooing to the baby they'd made together for a long, poignant moment in time.

"I love you," Dak said softly to Geris, his gaze finding hers. "Until we breathe our last breath, there will never be another love for me but you."

Geris smiled through her tears. "I love you too," she whispered.

"Forever?"

"Oh yeah." She searched his eyes. "Forever."

Epilogue

In a few hours time they would name the baby Jana, after Dak's dearly departed *mani*. Jana, who looked every inch her father's daughter, would grow to be like her mother in both temperament and spirit. A fact Dak would often boast about to others over the years.

Jana grew up to be both beautiful and strong, a woman who believed in loyalty, devotion, and the keeping of one's word. A daughter they could both be proud of.

Throughout the years more babies would be added to the household on Ti Q'won, each of them loved, each of them doted on, and each of them treasured equally. Their firstborn son Dar would grow to become a feared warlord and great king, their daughter Dari beloved amongst their people in her own right. All of their children would grow to be strong and capable, a cut above the rest.

But always Jana was the firstborn. A reminder of how it had felt to discover for the first time just what it was this thing called life was all about.

Geris had no way of knowing at the time how important her eldest child was to be. She had no way of knowing that Jana's destiny lay in wait some twenty-five Yessat years ahead in a world none from Tryston even knew existed.

Nor could Yar'at have known as he lay abed on Ti Q'won recovering from the ten grueling years he'd spent in slavery, that the fates had more in store for him than an early death in the crystal silius mines. The giant had no way of comprehending at this moment in time that he, a man who had been thought a simpleton as a boy-child and sold by his own parents because of a speech impediment, had a destiny laying in wait within the swirling golden mass of the planet called Tryston.

But then that's the funny thing about fate. Whether or not you choose to believe in destiny, it's always there, biding its time...

Waiting, and preparing to make itself known.

* * * * *

Next in the series:

NO MERCY

ISBN # 0-9724377-4-6

Giselle McKenzie trembled inexplicably as the sound of a low growl reverberated throughout the threads of her consciousness. She knew it couldn't have emitted from her date, the man sitting across from her in the quaint restaurant. Yet every time he placed his hand over hers, she heard that eerie, primitive growl...

Ellora's Cave Publishing
www.ellorascave.com

About the author:

Critically acclaimed and highly prolific, Jaid Black is the best-selling author of numerous erotic romance tales. Her first title, *The Empress' New Clothes*, was recognized as a readers' favorite in women's erotica by Romantic Times magazine. A full-time writer, Jaid lives in a cozy little village in the northeastern United States with her two children. In her spare time, she enjoys traveling, horseback riding, and furthering her collection of African and Egyptian art.

She welcomes mail from readers. You can write to her c/o Ellora's Cave Publishing at P.O. Box 787, Hudson, Ohio 44236-0787.

Why an electronic book?

We live in the Information Age — an exciting time in the history of human civilization in which technology rules supreme and continues to progress in leaps and bounds every minute of every hour of every day. For a multitude of reasons, more and more avid literary fans are opting to purchase e-books instead of paperbacks. The question to those not yet initiated to the world of electronic reading is simply: why?

1. Price. An electronic title at Ellora's Cave Publishing runs anywhere from 40-75% less than the cover price of the <u>exact same title</u> in paperback format. Why? Cold mathematics. It is less expensive to publish an e-book than it is to publish a paperback, so the savings are passed along to the consumer.

2. Space. Running out of room to house your paperback books? That is one worry you will never have with electronic novels. For a low one-time cost, you can purchase a handheld computer designed specifically for e-reading purposes. Many e-readers are larger than the average handheld, giving you plenty of screen room. Better yet, hundreds of titles can be stored within your new library — a single microchip. (Please note that Ellora's Cave does not endorse any specific brands. You can check our website at www.ellorascave.com under "how to read an e-book" for customer recommendations we make available to new consumers.)

3. Mobility. Because your new library now consists of only a microchip, your entire cache of books can be taken with you wherever you go.

4. Personal preferences are accounted for. Are the words you are currently reading too small? Too large? Too...**ANNOYING**? Paperback books cannot be modified according to personal preferences, but e-books can.

5. Innovation. The way you read a book is not the only advancement the Information Age has gifted the literary community with. There is also the factor of what you can read. Ellora's Cave Publishing will be introducing a new line of interactive titles that are available in e-book format only.

6. Instant gratification. Is it the middle of the night and all the bookstores are closed? Are you tired of waiting days—sometimes weeks—for online and offline bookstores to ship the novels you bought? Ellora's Cave Publishing sells instantaneous downloads 24 hours a day, 7 days a week, 365 days a year. Our e-book delivery system is 100% automated, meaning your order is filled as soon as you pay for it.

Those are a few of the top reasons why electronic novels are displacing paperbacks for many an avid reader. As always, Ellora's Cave Publishing welcomes your questions and comments. We invite you to email us at service@ellorascave.com or write to us directly at: P.O. Box 787, Hudson, Ohio 44236-0787.

The following excerpt from *The Possession*, © Jaid Black, 2002, is available in e-book format at www.ellorascave.com or in paperback anywhere Ellora's Cave books are sold. (ISBN # 0-9724377-6-2)

Prologue

Kris Torrence took a deep, contemplative breath as she stared at herself in the mirror of her postage stamp sized bathroom. *This can't be as good as it gets*, she thought morosely. *I can't be as good as I get...*

She was pretty enough, she supposed, with her wine-red hair and cat-like green eyes. Undoubtedly more average than beautiful but pretty enough that she should have been dating, should have been leading a more exciting life. Yet she wasn't and didn't.

Thirty-four and never married, Kris was content with being single—enjoyed it even. She liked living alone, relished the freedom of being able to do what she wanted when she wanted to do it without having to confer with a man about her plans for the evening. Being single definitely has its rewards.

But, she conceded, it has its drawbacks too.

Loneliness was the biggest of them. Lots and lots of lonely nights spent staring at the empty pillow next to hers in the queen-sized bed, fantasizing about falling in love, fantasizing about risqué sexual situations she'd realistically never find herself in. She was a normal woman after all. *She had needs.*

But mostly, she sighed, mostly she just fantasized about companionship.

However, she reminded herself, her chin going up a notch, she wasn't lonely for companionship altogether, just lonely for male companionship. And, she thought pointedly as her cat Hercules sauntered from the bathroom and toward the kitchen with a *meeow*, human male companionship in particular.

She winced, wondering not for the first time if she had inadvertently turned into the living portrait of an old maid without even realizing it. Hercules, she thought grimly, was but one of a grand total of five felines living in her apartment.

Five cats! Kris grimaced. When in the hell had she managed to acquire five cats? It's as if she'd fallen asleep one night a young woman and woke up the next morning a pathetic spinster.

She rolled her eyes at herself in the mirror. "Stop it, Kris," she chastised her image. "You're not a spinster and you know it. You're just..." She sighed. "...you're just lonely and bored."

It was the truth and she knew it. Yes, she was thirty-four. Yes, she had never been married. No, she wasn't dating anyone and hadn't in at least six months.

But overall she loved her life. She enjoyed her tenured position as a professor of anthropology at San Francisco State University, found the research she did on other cultures with her graduate students invigorating and challenging.

And, she sniffed, there was nothing wrong with owning cats. Many cats. Lots of cats. All kinds of cats. Smallish short-haired ones, tall and lanky long-haired ones, big fat furball ones, and—

Her teeth gritted. Okay, so maybe she owned too many goddamned cats.

But other than the fact she was a one-woman humane society, there wasn't anything wrong with her life and she knew it. And really, she thought with a grin as Zeus jumped up on the bathroom sink and purred against her hand while his rough tongue lapped at her skin there, there wasn't anything wrong with being a hopeless, dyed in the wool, lover of felines. It's just that...

Her grin slowly faded as she stared at herself in the mirror. It's just that she was a bit tired of the status quo, a bit tired of leading a boring, complacent existence.

And, she acknowledged as she drew in a deep breath, she had needs like any other normal woman. She was at her sexual peak for goodness sake—hardly the time in her life to remain celibate due to complacency!

She wanted to once—*just once*—do something wild and crazy, something completely out of character from the Dr. Kris Torrence everyone at the university knew and respected. Something brazen and reckless enough to give her a lifetime of memories she could hug close to her heart whenever she was in the mood to wax sentimental on rebellious days gone by. She was getting older and...

She sighed. In her youth, and onward into her twenties, she had always done the right thing, the proper thing. As a teenager she had done what the nuns at the parochial school she'd attended had expected of her, she had been the good girl her parents had wanted her to be, and...

And she was sick as she didn't know what of being that good girl. No thirty-four year-old woman needs to conform to the expectations of others when those expectations were not her own. Or, more to the point, no thirty-four year-old woman *should* conform to the expectations of others when those expectations were not her own.

Kris nibbled at her lower lip as her eyes slowly strayed down to the bathroom sink counter and toward the magazine laying opened on it. She mentally resisted rereading the classified ad she'd been compelled to study for what felt like a thousand times in the past three days. But in the end she found her hands reaching for it and her heart rate picking up as her eyes soaked in the words:

Hotel Atlantis is currently searching for select females to work in our exclusive gentlemen's resort situated on a private island off the coast of San Francisco. Pay is exceptional for exceptional females as our resort accommodates only the wealthiest of clientele. Women comfortable in the role of submissive are especially needed. Island excursions last anywhere from 3-7 days...

Kris blew out a breath as she reread the part of the ad that most appealed to her.

Women comfortable in the role of submissive are especially needed.

It had always been a fantasy, she conceded as she chewed on her bottom lip. A very big, got-her-wet-every-time-she-thought-about-it fantasy...

To be submissive to a man. To play slave to his master. To allow a man to tie her up and do anything he wanted to her—

It was something no good girl would do.

It was something she wanted to do very badly.

Her heartbeat sped up. *Just for one night*, she promised herself. *Or in this case, just for one island excursion.*

It wasn't as if nobody had ever heard of Hotel Atlantis. On the contrary, everybody who lived in or around the Bay area knew precisely what the resort was and whom the resort catered to, even if it wasn't the sort of topic one tended to bring up in casual conversation.

Hotel Atlantis was *the* exclusive place that elite businessmen went for sun, fun, and no-strings-attached sex with any paid woman, and as many paid women, of their choosing.

If you want to live out your deepest sexual fantasies without anybody of your acquaintance finding out about it, this would be the place to do it, Kris. She took another deep breath. *There is no way in hell that any of your male colleagues at the university make enough money to frequent that island!*

Kris set the magazine down on the bathroom sink counter and resumed staring at herself in the mirror. She doubted such an exclusive gentlemen's retreat as Hotel Atlantis would want to hire a woman as average looking as she was anyway. But maybe if she let her long and curly wine-red hair down from the bun, and applied a little bit of make-up, and…

Her lips pinched together in a frown. Perhaps if she underwent a complete reconstructive overhaul of her average face she could talk Hotel Atlantis into letting her work one excursion.

She bristled at that. As if she wanted to work in a place where she was destined to be the ugliest woman on the entire island! Especially, she thought morosely, when the entire reason she wanted to go in the first place wasn't for the money as the other women no doubt were, but to get a little action.

She sighed as she glanced back down at the ad.

Hotel Atlantis will be conducting in-person interviews throughout the entire last week of March in the San Francisco area. Call John Calder today at 555-3212 to —

She stopped reading, her finger tracing the outline of the printed telephone number. "On the other hand," she murmured, "it can't hurt to at least call the guy."

Closing her eyes briefly and taking a steadying breath, she shut the magazine and slowly turned around to face the exit to the bathroom.

Nervous and feeling surprisingly giddy, Kris swallowed hard in her throat as she found herself walking toward the kitchen — and the telephone. When she reached it, when the cordless phone's receiver was firmly in hand, she took a deep breath before pounding out the telephone number she'd committed to memory three days ago.

"This is insane," she muttered to herself as she waited for someone on the other end of the line to pick up. "I must have lost my — "

"Thank you for calling Hotel Atlantis. This is Sheri Carucci. How may I assist you this evening?"

Kris's green eyes widened at the disembodied sound of the throaty voice. Her heartbeat picked up so dramatically that she idly wondered for one hysterical moment if it would come thumping out of her chest.

"Hello? This is Hotel Atlantis. Hello?"

Her breathing grew labored as her heartbeat climbed impossibly higher.

"Very funny, buddy. Listen," the throaty-turned-annoyed voice asked, "you wanna book a stay on the island or not?"

Terrified, and feeling way out of her element, Kris's hand flew to the wall console, preparing to hang up. But just as she was about to end the connection, just as her fingers were about to press the disconnect button, her gaze was snagged by a photograph hanging on the wall a foot away.

Her eyes narrowed into slits. The photograph was of herself and her five cats.

If only I had been wearing a parochial schoolgirl uniform in that picture the pathetic good girl imagery would be complete!

Kris's nostrils flared as she planted her hand firmly on her hip so it couldn't fly up to the disconnect button of its own accord and nervously end the connection with Madame Throaty Voice against her volition.

"My name is Kris," she determinedly gritted out into the receiver, her chin thrusting up. And with the conviction and resolution of a recovering alcoholic at a group prevention meeting, she added loudly and cathartically, her nostrils flaring impossibly further, "and I'm a submissive!"

"Hold on a sec," Madame Throaty Voice replied with a yawn. "Let me transfer you upstairs to that department."

Kris grunted.